FERN G. BROWN

Weekly Reader Books presents

JOCKEY-or Else!

Illustrated by Darrell Wiskur

Albert Whitman & Company, Chicago

This book is for Bud and Lee.

This book is a presentation of Weekly Reader Books.
Weekly Reader Books offers book clubs for children from
preschool to young adulthood. All quality hardcover books are selected
by a distinguished Weekly Reader Selection Board.

For further information write to:
Weekly Reader Books
1250 Fairwood Ave.
Columbus, Ohio 43216

Library of Congress Cataloging in Publication Data

Brown, Fern.
    Jockey—or else!

    (Pilot books)
    SUMMARY: His summer experiences at Lakeside
Horse Farm convince Benjy he will never be a
jockey, therefore he sets more realistic goals that
will still involve him with horses.
    [1. Horses—Fiction] I. Wiskur, Darrell D.
II. Title.
PZ7.B81356Jo   [Fic]   78-1715
ISBN 0-8075-3944-9

Text © 1978 by Fern G. Brown
Illustrations © by Albert Whitman & Company
Published simultaneously in Canada by
George J. McLeod, Limited, Toronto
All rights reserved. Printed in U.S.A.

The authors and editors gratefully acknowledge the assistance given in preparing this book by the following: Mary Brown, ornithologist and director of Brown's Bird Hospital, Chicago, Illinois; Tom Mick, judge approved by the American Quarter Horse Association, Appaloosa Horse Club, and Paint Horse Associations; T.N. Phillips, D.V.M. of the Illinois Equine Hospital and Clinic, Naperville, Illinois; Arthur A. Thompson, former jockey, riding master, horse trainer, and presently stall superintendent at Arlington Park Race Track, Arlington Park, Illinois; Leonard J. Brown, Arlene Duda, Frances Lindstrom, and Marion Markham for manuscript assistance.

Contents

1
Lakeside Horse Farm

THE STREET in front of the Braeburn bus station was empty. Benjy dropped his duffel bag and carefully put down the bird carrier on the sidewalk. The black crow inside picked at the wire mesh.

"Don't worry, Arcaro," Benjy said to the bird he'd named after his idol, jockey Eddie Arcaro. "They haven't forgotten us."

"You bet! You bet!" came the crow's scratchy voice.

"Good boy. Someone will be here soon."

"You bet!" squawked Arcaro.

Benjy sat on his bag and waited.

A bright blue pickup truck stopped at the curb. Benjy leaped up, and his foot caught in the duffel bag cord. He sprawled on the sidewalk.

"Are you hurt?" called the driver.

"Naw," said Benjy, getting to his feet. "I just tripped." When he was excited, Benjy sometimes couldn't control his arms and legs.

A bald man jumped out. He was so short that his eyes were level with Benjy's.

"Are you Benjy Tennen?"

Benjy nodded.

The man put out his hand. "I'm Jim Spear."

Benjy felt a shiver of excitement as he shook hands with the famous jockey.

Benjy had heard about Jim Spear at the Youth Club in Chicago. Bud Goldberg, the club leader, had told him that Jim trained young people to become jockeys. Benjy's parents had made arrangements for Benjy to spend the summer working and taking riding lessons at Jim's horse farm on the outskirts of the city. Benjy paid half of the room and board with money he'd earned from his part-time job. His parents paid the rest.

Jim looked Benjy over, from the worn toes of his cowboy boots to the visor of his faded red cap. "So you want to be a jockey."

"Yes, sir!"

Becoming a jockey was the most important thing in the world to Benjy. He thought about it all day in school. He thought about it while he worked in the bird hospital on weekends. Now, amazing as it seemed, he'd take riding lessons from Jim Spear. Jim had a good reputation for developing riders.

"Ever been on a horse?" Jim asked.

"Yes," said Benjy. "Last summer I helped the carnival man give horseback rides. He let me ride his horses. He said I was the right size and weight for a jockey."

Jim smiled. "Danny Hoffman, the last boy we had with us, is a big-time jockey now. But Danny was a natural."

"Maybe I'm a natural."

"I certainly hope so, Benjy. We'll soon find out." Jim picked up Benjy's duffel bag. "Hop in," he said. Benjy grabbed the bird carrier and Jim asked, "What's that?"

"Arcaro, my pet crow. He goes where I go. Okay?"

"Okay. I like his name," Jim said, laughing. He threw the bag into the truck and climbed behind the wheel. Benjy wriggled into the seat beside Jim.

On the way to the farm Jim said, "I'm a trainer at the racetrack now." He patted his stomach. "Just a bit plump and past the age to be a jockey."

Benjy leaned forward in his seat. "Is thirteen a good age for a jockey?"

"Thirteen is a good age to start training, but…"

Benjy sighed and sat back. He didn't want to hear any "buts." Eddie Arcaro was thirteen when he got his first racetrack job.

As they drove along the highway, Jim told about

the horse farm. "I buy sick or lame animals that would probably be put to death because they can't work at the track any more."

"Do you make 'em well?" Benjy asked.

"Yep. That's the idea."

"And then do they race again?"

"Oh, no. Their legs will never be strong enough for racing. But because an animal isn't strong enough to race doesn't mean it can't live a useful life. We retrain most of our horses for pleasure riding."

The truck turned off the highway onto a gravel road, past a sign that said "Fertilizer for Sale." Jim pointed to the sign. "I sell manure and get carrots for the horses with the money. I always say that my horses buy their own carrots."

Benjy laughed. He knew he was going to like Jim Spear.

They turned a corner, and Benjy saw a green world of grassy rolling hills and lush meadows. A sweet smell filled the air, reminding him of the doughnut shop near his apartment house in Chicago. That must be the grass, he thought. Benjy was used to cement streets.

Jim stopped the truck at a rambling white farmhouse with a blue door. He honked and got out. Benjy followed, carrying Arcaro. The blue door swung open, and a woman and two teenagers came out. Jim said, "Benjy, meet my family. Linda, my wife, and Sherri and Paul."

"Hello, Mrs. Spear," said Benjy.

"We're informal here, Benjy—call us by our first names," Linda Spear said, pushing short auburn hair away from her eyes. "Welcome to Lakeside Farm." Linda was taller than her husband and wore jeans and a blue T-shirt.

There was a moment's silence. Linda looked at the boy and girl behind her. "Paul? Sherri?"

Sherri held out her hand. "Hi, Benjy." She was about his age, and her smile was warm. She seemed like someone who could be a good friend.

Paul, a chunky redhead of perhaps fifteen, had cool gray eyes. His brows drew together in a scowl, and his mouth formed a straight line. He looked at Benjy and said "Hullo" as if it hurt him to say it.

Before Benjy could figure out why Paul was scowling, Jim said, "Benjy, you'll bunk in Paul's room. There's an extra twin bed."

"Yeh, Danny's bed," mumbled Paul.

Benjy remembered that Danny was the boy who had made it as a jockey.

Jim said, "Benjy, Paul will show you your bed. I'll be back soon to show you around."

Paul picked up the duffel bag with a curt nod. Carrying Arcaro, Benjy followed him upstairs. Sherri tagged along.

"What's in there?" Sherri asked, pointing to the carrier.

"Arcaro, my pet crow."

"Can I see him?"

"Sure." When they reached Paul's room, Benjy opened the mesh door. Arcaro flew out and perched on Benjy's shoulder.

"Where did you get him?" asked Sherri.

"At the bird hospital when he was just a baby."

"He's pretty. The sun makes his coat look like a rainbow."

"He's smart, too. Arcaro can talk and do lots of things," Benjy boasted.

"Make him say something," demanded Paul.

Benjy put out his hand and Arcaro perched on it. "Hi, boy. Are you happy?"

Arcaro flew around the room, then settled on the top of his carrier.

"C'mon, say 'you bet!'" Benjy urged.

Paul gave a nasty laugh.

Arcaro hopped on Benjy's shoulder. His black eyes darted nervously. He didn't even say caw.

"He's shy in front of other people," said Benjy. "He always talks when we're alone."

Sherri said, "Maybe he'll talk when he gets to know us."

"You're some bird trainer." Paul's voice was a sneer. "I hope you're better with horses."

Benjy put his clothes into the drawers. He took out his scrapbook and Eddie Arcaro's book, *I Ride to Win!* and placed them carefully on the dresser.

Paul said, "Danny was great. He knew all about animals, especially horses. He's at the racetrack this minute, riding the best horses."

Benjy clenched his fist. He wanted to punch Paul and shut him up. But he remembered what Bud Goldberg, his Youth Club leader, had said. "It's okay to fight for your rights, but not with fists." He'd better not fight and spoil his chances to be a jockey. But Benjy promised himself silently that he'd show Paul. Someday he'd be a better jockey than Danny ever was!

Paul went on. "Danny lived here for three years. Dad trained him. He slept in this very bed."

Jim Spear stuck his head in. "Ready, Benjy? When you've made up your bunk, meet me at the corral. Sherri, it's your turn to set the table."

Paul smiled. "Go ahead, Benjy," he said. "I'll make up your bed."

Benjy couldn't believe his ears—Paul was going to be friendly, after all. Benjy was glad he hadn't picked a fight. Bud Goldberg had been right.

"Thanks, Paul," Benjy said. "'Bye, Sherri." With Arcaro on his shoulder, Benjy headed out the door.

2
Trouble Seeker

JIM GAVE BENJY a tour of the farm. Horses grazed in a field, and at one end there was a little lake where water lilies grew. Pointing to a small blue barn, Jim said, "Privately owned horses are kept there. Paul takes care of our eight boarders."

They walked to a large blue barn and Jim explained, "No red barns for us. Linda loves the color blue, and everything she wears is blue."

The hinges of the barn door creaked, and the horses nickered a welcome when they heard Jim's voice. The smell of manure and leather hit Benjy. But he didn't mind. He liked being with the horses and hearing his boot heels click on the wooden planking.

Benjy counted six stalls on each side of the barn.

"Sherri's aisle is on the right," Jim said. "These horses on the left will be yours to feed and care for.

There are only five now. A new horse is coming in from the track tomorrow."

A Thoroughbred chestnut gelding with a white star on his forehead was in the first stall. He stuck out his head and nudged off Benjy's cap. Arcaro fussed and fluttered to Benjy's other shoulder. Benjy picked up the hat. The horse whinnied.

"Which horse is this?" Benjy asked.

"Trouble Seeker," said Jim. "And he lives up to his name. I was his trainer at the racetrack. He ran in $20,000 stake races until his legs broke down. His owner was going to destroy him."

Benjy wondered who could think of destroying this beautiful horse with the long chestnut mane and tail. "I'm glad you didn't let them."

"I hate to see a horse die. I bought him, and we've nursed him for over a year. Linda is going to retrain him for pleasure riding. Racehorses are edgy and excitable. They must be taught to relax, not compete."

"Can I ride him?"

"Not at first. He's for experienced riders. But I'll give you lessons on Socks. He's a good horse and dependable for beginners. We'll start soon."

Benjy patted Trouble's white star, and the horse nickered. Benjy felt as if he'd made a new friend.

Jim showed the boy other horses. Cherokee was a brown-and-white pinto, thirty years old. He was called a lead pony. But he wasn't really a pony. Jim explained that at a racetrack all horses that aren't racers are called ponies.

Jim rubbed Cherokee's nose. "This old fellow was Paul's first horse. He's been around a long time. Paul still brings him a treat every day."

Benjy liked all of Jim's horses, but Trouble Seeker was his favorite.

"Sherri will show you what we feed the horses. We feed early in the morning before our breakfast. There's lots to do—groom horses, shine gear, muck out stalls. We'll probably paint the barns this summer. But we'll also ride, go on picnics, swim, have horse shows and parades. I hope you'll like it here."

"Oh, I do already. I want to be a jockey more than anything."

"First, the basics, and then if you have the stuff, we'll start you as a groom or exercise boy. You don't become a jockey overnight."

"What if I'm a natural like Danny?"

Jim smiled. "It took Danny three years, remember."

A loud gong interrupted Jim. "There's the dinner bell. Let's go. Linda doesn't like us to be late."

Soon after dinner cleanup, Paul began to yawn. Benjy was tired, too. It had been an exciting day.

Paul was in bed before Benjy put Arcaro on his perch for the night and switched off the light. Benjy tried to get his legs under the covers. His toes stubbed on something hard and cold.

"Ouch! My toes!" he gasped. His leg brushed against something slimy. A snake!

Benjy yanked the blanket and sheets and sent stones flying in every direction. He switched on the lamp. On the floor was something long and green. Not a snake, but a slimy water lily stem. This was why Paul had offered to make Benjy's bed.

Paul was laughing so hard that tears ran down his cheeks. "So superstar is afraid of a little water lily," he said.

That did it! Maybe Benjy wasn't a horseman like Danny, but he knew how to fight. He jumped at Paul, who slid backward out of bed, knocking over the lamp. As Paul began to get up, Benjy pulled him down. The boys wrestled on the floor, gasping and grunting.

Benjy rolled on top of Paul and tried to pin him. Paul escaped and threw Benjy against a table. Arcaro squawked "Caw! Caw!" and flew around the room.

Jim's voice called, "What's going on in there?"

Benjy sat up and tried to catch his breath.

Paul, breathing hard, wiped his nose on his pajama sleeve. "Just fooling around, Dad."

"Well, cool it and get some sleep. Six o'clock comes mighty early."

"Okay. We're going to bed now." Paul shook his fist at Benjy and slipped under the covers.

Benjy, chest heaving, picked up his sheets and blanket and then threw the stones in the wastebasket. He straightened his bed and crawled in. There was no sound from Paul. Just let Paul Spear keep pushing me, Benjy thought, and he's in for a big surprise.

The gong awakened Benjy the next morning. He rubbed his eyes and looked around the room. Paul's bed was made, and he was gone. "Good!" Benjy said aloud. "I can get along without that creep."

"You bet!" said Arcaro.

"Arcaro! Why wouldn't you talk yesterday in front of Paul and Sherri?"

The crow flew about the room, and Benjy said, "Six o'clock. I'd better feed my horses."

While he dressed and made his bed, Arcaro called, "Ben-nn-njy! Six o'clock!" just the way his mother did every school morning at home.

Arcaro's voice was harsh and raspy, but the tone reminded Benjy of his mom. It made him homesick for his parents and their crowded apartment. He'd write them tonight.

"Ben-nn-njy!" cawed Arcaro.

18

"Okay," Benjy said.

"Okay," Arcaro repeated.

Benjy and the crow went out to the barn.

Sherri was in the feed room surrounded by sacks, cans, and barrels. Arcaro perched on a bale of hay. He cocked his head but said nothing.

"Morning," said Benjy.

"Oh, hi." Sherri waved a feed scoop in greeting. "I'm fixing breakfast. We've got oats, Omalene, bran, corn, and linseed pellets. Every horse gets a different mixture."

"How do I know what to feed my horses?"

"The ration for each horse is posted on his door. Dad watches carefully to see that the horses maintain their weight. If not, he changes the feed."

Benjy walked over to Trouble Seeker's stall. The chestnut Thoroughbred kicked the door.

He's hungry, thought Benjy. He patted the white star. "Just a minute, big boy, I'm new at this."

When Benjy stooped to read the chart on the door, Trouble Seeker nudged off his cap. "You got me again!" Benjy laughed. "Now don't kick, I'll be right back with your breakfast."

Sherri taught Benjy how to mix the rations, and he watched her fill the water buckets in her stalls. Then Benjy took the hose and watered his horses. Old Cherokee licked the bucket.

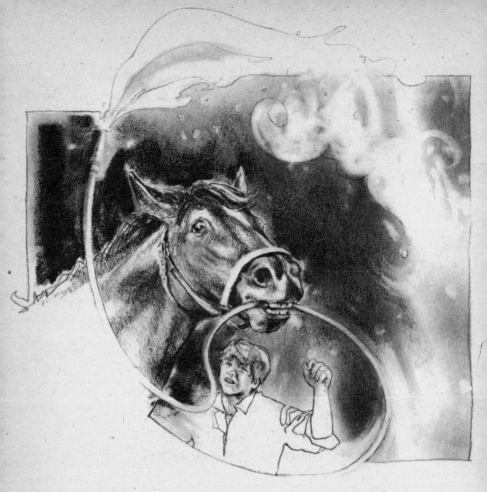

Benjy, holding the hose, slid open the door of
Trouble Seeker's stall and moved toward the water
bucket. Before Benjy knew what was happening,
Trouble grabbed the hose with his teeth.

With a tug, Benjy got the hose free, but he lost
his balance and fell. The hose spewed water on
Trouble Seeker, the walls, the nearby horses, on
Benjy's hair, face, and shirt.

Before Benjy could stop him, Trouble Seeker

was through the door and loping out of the barn.

"Sherri! Catch him!" Benjy yelled.

"Caw! Caw!" shrieked Arcaro, flying around the barn and adding to the confusion.

Sherri grabbed a lead rope and raced after Trouble Seeker. By the time Benjy was on his feet and had turned off the water, Sherri was back, leading Trouble Seeker. The horse didn't seem a bit sorry. Benjy thought he noticed a funny gleam in Trouble Seeker's eye.

"Man, am I glad you found him," Benjy said.

"Oh, no problem. Trouble Seeker always runs down to the fence near the lake." Sherri opened the stall door, and Trouble walked in. "He used to munch the flowers and trees until the neighbors complained."

"They probably don't like horses."

"You can say that again." Sherri's pigtails bobbed up and down, and her eyes were serious. "Trouble Seeker and the other horses ate a dozen or so of Mrs. Salamon's dahlias, ripped the bark off some young maple trees, and nibbled her prize roses—all in one day."

"No wonder she doesn't like horses."

"Mrs. Salamon wanted to call a lawyer."

"Gosh, that would be bad for your dad."

"Dad apologized and replaced all the flowers and trees. Then he built a high stockade fence so the horses can't reach over. But Trouble Seeker still loves to go there."

"Well, he'd better not!"

"Mrs. Salamon says that if it happens again, she'll ask the village council to ban horses in Braeburn."

The gong sounded.

Sherri wiped her hands on her jeans. "Breakfast. C'mon, we can wash up at the house."

Benjy called Arcaro, but the crow stayed behind in the barn. As he and Sherri left, Benjy heard the horses munching at their feed bins. It was a pleasant sound. He liked caring for the horses at Lakeside so much. If only it weren't for...

Sherri broke into his thoughts. "Paul's cooking breakfast today. We all take turns."

So that's where he'd gone this morning, thought Benjy. Although his stomach was sending him hunger messages, he wasn't looking forward to seeing Paul.

The kitchen smelled of coffee and bacon. Jim and Linda were already seated at the large wooden trestle table. They smiled and said good morning.

Paul stood at the stove, scrambling eggs. He didn't look up.

Jim said, "Hope you don't mind that we didn't wait. I've got to get to the track early today."

Benjy sat down next to Jim. "That's okay."

22

"Linda's got a big day, too," Jim said. "She's going to begin retraining Trouble Seeker. Did you learn the ropes about feeding and watering?"

Benjy nodded, drinking orange juice.

"Any problems?" asked Jim.

Benjy looked at Sherri. She inspected her fingernails.

"No," he replied.

Linda said, "Do you think you could cook breakfast, Benjy?"

"Yes," he said. "I can even make pancakes."

"Good!" Linda wiped her mouth with a blue paper napkin. "Friday is your day. That means feeding the horses fifteen minutes earlier. You can make your own lunch whenever you're hungry."

Paul brought a plate of bacon and eggs for Sherri and one for Benjy. Benjy began to eat.

Linda said, "I make dinner every night. Except when Jim takes us out, which isn't too often."

Jim stood up. "That's my clue to leave. Good breakfast, Paul. Listen, everyone, watch for Jet, our new racehorse. She'll be arriving with Ed Krinn sometime this morning. Ed will need your help. Jet's lame. Put her in the stall next to Trouble Seeker for now."

Linda nodded, and Paul said, "We'll take care of her, Dad."

Jim was almost out the door when he turned and

said, "Sherri, will you show Benjy how to clean the stalls and groom horses? Benjy, your riding lesson will be at nine o'clock tomorrow morning."

"I can hardly wait," Benjy said. He wanted to show everyone, especially Paul, that he was a natural, like Danny.

After breakfast, Benjy learned how to muck out with the pitchfork and turn over the bedding in the stalls. When Trouble Seeker nudged him, Benjy shooed him away. "Oh, what large teeth you have, big boy!" Benjy laughed. "You're not grabbing my cap this time."

At the sound of Benjy's voice, Arcaro flew in, then disappeared again out the back door. The crow seemed to feel right at home around the barn.

Sherri said, "I have to groom and saddle Trouble Seeker for Mom. She'll be back from shopping soon."

"Can I help?" Benjy asked.

"Sure." Sherri tethered the horse in the aisle. "Trouble loves attention. I've been grooming him for several weeks."

Sherri taught Benjy to use the rubber curry-comb. She told him that the currycomb loosened the dirt in the horse's coat. Then she tapped the comb against her heel to clean it.

"Now we polish him," Sherri said. As she and Benjy rubbed Trouble Seeker gently with soft brushes, she explained. "I should pick Trouble's feet with a hoof pick, but he's touchy about the legs. Mom will do it."

When they had combed Trouble Seeker's chestnut mane and tail, Benjy stood back and admired him. "Hey, he's beautiful! I wish I could ride him."

Just then Paul came into the barn. "Why don't you?" he asked.

Benjy turned from Paul's challenging stare.

"Why don't you ride him, superstar?" Paul asked again.

"Paul! What's got into you?" Sherri said. "This horse hasn't been ridden in a year. He still thinks he's a racehorse. It'll take a lot of retraining before he's ready."

She straightened the pad, put the saddle on, and tightened the girth around Trouble Seeker.

Paul said, "Danny rode Julep without retraining."

"Danny was an exercise boy then, a good rider. And beside, Trouble's excitable. Remember how long it took to get him to stand still enough to put a saddle on? Trouble's not Julep."

"Danny's not afraid of any horse alive," stated Paul.

"Neither am I!" blurted Benjy. Suddenly he really wanted to ride Trouble Seeker.

He had to prove that he was as good as Danny. If he rode Trouble Seeker he'd be like Danny, maybe better, because Julep was a calm horse and Trouble wasn't.

Paul said, "I'll put the bridle on." He bridled the horse and led him outside.

Sherri stood near the barn. "Don't do it, Benjy," she warned.

Trouble Seeker shifted his weight nervously and tossed his head. He looked around the stable yard and snorted.

"I'll hold him while you get on," said Paul, motioning toward the mounting block. His cool, gray eyes dared Benjy to ride.

When Benjy climbed on the block, a shiver shook him. Even from up here, Trouble Seeker was a giant. The carnival man had taught Benjy to mount a horse on the left side, with the reins over the horse's neck. That was all that he knew about riding. But he couldn't back out now. Not if he was going to be like Danny. He wished that Sherri would stop him or that Linda would pull into the driveway. But Sherri was silent, and Linda's blue pickup was nowhere in sight.

3
A Sick Horse

TROUBLE SEEKER blew out a long breath and pawed the ground. When Benjy reached for the metal stirrup, the Thoroughbred's eyes flashed white.

"Easy, big boy," Benjy said, hoping to soothe the tense animal. He put his foot in the stirrup, swung the other leg over, and slid into the saddle.

Slowly Benjy gathered the reins. Trouble Seeker pranced a few quick side steps. Then he arched his neck, laid back his ears, and bucked. The sudden violent movement threw Benjy off balance, and he lost the stirrups. Trouble Seeker took off in a swirl of dust, and Benjy fell forward on the horse's neck, dropping the reins.

"Whoa!" cried Benjy. "Whoa!"

Trouble Seeker seemed to think that he was on

the racetrack, heading for the finish wire. He ran at full speed, reins dangling. Benjy clutched fistfuls of mane.

"Hang on!" yelled Sherri.

"You sure don't ride like Danny!" shouted Paul.

Trouble Seeker galloped through the yard, out of the gate, and into the pasture. Then he lowered his head, and charged the fence near the lake.

Benjy clenched his teeth so tightly that his ears hurt. The fence was coming closer. Although his legs flopped helplessly at the horse's sides, he didn't loosen his grip on Trouble's mane. He wanted to pick up the reins, but his fists wouldn't open. He tried yelling for help, but the cry started up his throat and stuck there.

Suddenly they were at the fence!

Benjy closed his eyes and braced himself for the impact. But Trouble Seeker looked up, made a swift turn to one side, and stopped. For Benjy, the stop was so unexpected that he lost his grip on the horse's mane and sailed over the fence, head first. The earth rushed toward him, and he landed in soft dirt.

Thorns pricked Benjy's neck. He struggled to a sitting position, his head throbbing. He was surrounded by rosebushes. Behind him, a girl's voice, high and excited, asked, "Are you all right? What happened?"

Benjy rubbed his neck. Then he looked around. The girl was younger than he, with short blonde hair and braces on her teeth. He tried to tell her that he was okay, but all he could do was nod. He sputtered out a mouthful of dirt and wiped his mouth on his sleeve.

"What happened?" the girl asked again.

Benjy moistened his lips. "I was riding a racehorse. He stopped—I didn't."

She gave a low whistle. "Any broken bones?"

"I don't think so. My head hurts a little, and my neck."

"Can you stand up?"

"I'll try." Benjy struggled to his feet.

"You must be new around here."

"I came to Lakeside Farm yesterday."

"Oh, you're Benjy. Sherri told me about you. I'm Mara Salamon."

Benjy remembered that *Salamon* was the name of the woman who hated horses.

Mara said, "I guess that Sherri also told you about my mother."

Benjy nodded.

"You'd better leave before she catches you here."

"Shouldn't I clean up this mess first?"

"I'll take care of the rosebushes after you've gone."

"How do I get out of here? I don't want your

29

mother to know that a horse dumped me over the fence. It might be bad for Jim and Linda."

"I've got a secret passage."

"Where?"

"I haven't shown it to anyone. My mother would kill me if she knew I sneaked around to Lakeside." Mara looked over her shoulder. When she was satisfied that no one was watching, she walked to a large rosebush near the fence. Benjy saw a tunnel under the fence, the kind a dog might dig.

"Crawl under here," Mara said.

Benjy took a step forward and hesitated. The space seemed too small.

"Go ahead," she urged. "I do it every day. And you're not much bigger than I am."

"Thanks." Benjy gave a little wave, then got down on his stomach.

"Bye," Mara said. "See you later."

After scrunching up his knees, Benjy crawled through. The back of his shirt scraped the fence and ripped just as he reached the other side. He couldn't bother about his shirt because he heard Sherri calling, "Benjy! Benjy!"

"Here," he shouted, getting to his feet. The knees of his jeans were black with mud.

Sherri was puffing. "Are you okay?" She touched his arm. "Mom drove in right after

Trouble Seeker took off. Was she ever mad! Trouble went wild. We've been chasing him all over the place and looking for you!"

Benjy frowned. "Riding Trouble Seeker was a dumb idea."

"It sure was."

"Is he all right?"

Sherri nodded. "He's in the stall now. How about you? Are you hurt?"

"No. I'm used to falling. But I shouldn't have done it."

"Yeh. C'mon."

As they walked toward the barn, Benjy saw a large red van heading for the farm driveway. The words "Caution—Horses" stood out in big white letters on the side of the truck.

"That's the van bringing our new horse," said Sherri. "I'll tell Mom you're okay"

Sherri went into the large blue barn and returned with her mother and Paul.

Linda's face was flushed. "Benjy, I'm glad you're all right, but you had no business riding that horse," she said sternly. "You might have been killed. And now Trouble Seeker won't calm down."

"I'm sorry," Benjy said, very low.

Paul laughed. "Hey, superstar, racehorses aren't merry-go-round ponies!"

"That's enough, Paul," his mother said. "Benjy, don't ever ride again without permission. Understand?"

Benjy nodded. He felt awful for making Linda angry. As for Paul, if it took all summer, he was going to show the big ape that he was as good a rider as Danny.

"Okay," Linda said, "let's forget about it. Ed is here, and we have to see to Jet."

Arcaro flew around the yard and perched on Benjy's shoulder. When Benjy paid no attention to him, he cawed loudly.

Ed Krinn called, "Hi, Linda, hi, kids. Where do you want the mare?"

"In the big barn. We've got a clean stall ready," Linda replied.

"I'll pull up closer," said Ed. "This mare's in a bad way."

When Ed started the motor, the noise disturbed Arcaro. He fussed and fluttered his wings and hid in a nearby tree. Ed backed the van as near as possible to the barn door and jumped out. "I'll need your help, Linda. Paul's, too. Jet's heavily sedated. Dr. Egel gave her a shot to kill the pain. She can barely walk."

Ed opened the van door, lowered the tailgate ramp, and gently turned Jet around. She was a sleek black Thoroughbred. The red halter she wore set off her dark mane. Her right front leg was in a cast.

"Paul, hold up the bad leg above the cast," said Ed. "That's right. Now Linda, grab her halter." Ed put his body against the horse's shoulder opposite the bad leg to help maintain balance. "Okay, let's move," he directed.

Very slowly, the three inched their way down the ramp with the new horse. Jet leaned heavily for support, almost hopping on three legs.

Paul was sweating. "Man, is she ever heavy!"

At the sound of his voice Jet pointed her ears and turned her head as if to ask, "Where am I?" Her brown eyes had a dazed look.

Benjy and Sherri ran to open the barn door as the three approached with the horse. Trouble Seeker banged on his stall when he saw the new horse. Even old Cherokee looked out to see what was going on.

Finally, Benjy slid open Jet's stall door, and the mare was safely led inside.

Ed wiped his forehead with a red checked handkerchief. "Take good care of her. She doesn't have a mean bone in her body," he said.

Linda assured Ed that Jet would be all right.

After Ed left, Jet stood quietly at the open stall door, keeping her weight off her bad leg. She didn't show any interest in the full feed bin.

Sherri asked, "What happened to Jet's leg?"

"She hurt it in a race, and it became infected," said Linda. "It's in a plaster cast now."

"Poor old gal," said Sherri.

"She's not that old," Linda said. "Only nine. She's won a quarter of a million dollars."

Linda gently rubbed the horse's neck. "When Jim heard that her owner was going to send her to a dog food canning factory, he couldn't bear it."

Benjy drew in a quick breath. "Will she get well?"

Linda shrugged. "We don't know. The infection is pretty bad. She'll probably always swing that leg. Let's see if we can get her to drink some water."

A horn honked in the yard. Paul looked out. "It's Lori Oostdyke and Sara Morris," he said. "Let's go, Sherri."

"They board their horses here," Sherri explained. "We help them get ready for lessons."

Sherri and Paul left, and Benjy stayed behind with Linda. He wanted to get the sick horse to drink.

"Have a nice, cool drink of water, Jet," he urged. "It'll do you good." He stroked her nose.

Trouble Seeker snorted in the next stall. "Don't be jealous, Trouble. I didn't forget you," Benjy said. "But I've got to help Jet drink."

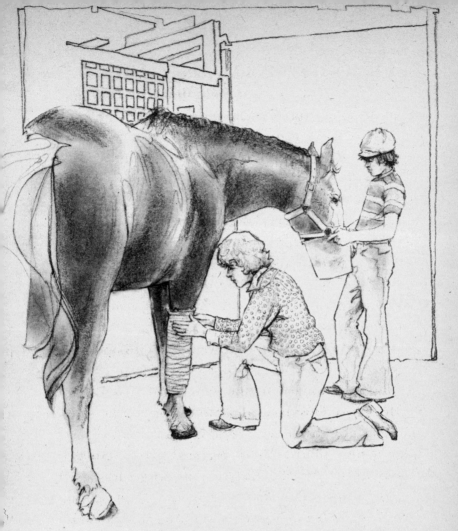

Again he urged the sick mare toward the bucket. Her suffering brown eyes looked at Benjy, then at the water bucket. He unhooked the bucket, brought it to her, and splashed water on her mouth. She dipped her head, licked around the bucket, and took a long swallow.

Linda smiled. "Jet trusts you."

"I like taking care of sick animals. In Chicago I worked in a bird hospital."

"Oh, that's right. I forgot. We were thinking of moving Jet to Sherri's side of the barn. I didn't know if you could handle her."

"Oh, please keep her in my aisle."

"Paul and Sherri like working with horses, but they haven't much patience with sick ones."

"I'll take good care of Jet," Benjy begged.

Linda bit her lip. "It'll be six weeks before the cast comes off."

"Please!"

"Well, she seems happy here with you. All right."

"Do you mean it?"

"Of course I mean it. The vet will give her shots every morning, one for the infection, the other to kill the pain. Follow his orders. You'll need lots of patience. No decisions before clearing with Jim or me. Understand?"

Benjy felt his face get warm. Linda was probably thinking about his ride on Trouble Seeker. He said, "I understand."

Linda sighed softly as she slid the stall door closed. "Jet was a great racehorse. I hope she makes it."

4
Trouble Seeker Is Tamed

THE NEXT MORNING Benjy and Sherri were in the barn with Jet when Jim came in. "How's the mare?" he asked.

Sherri sighed. "She won't eat."

"She still seems to be in pain, even after the shots," said Benjy.

Jim pursed his lips. "It takes time for the painkiller to work." He slid open the stall door. "Let me see your leg, Jet." But the horse retreated and wouldn't let Jim touch her.

Benjy slipped inside, keeping close to the wall. "C'mon, let Jim have a look," he said in a low voice. The mare's frightened brown eyes met his. Benjy came closer and held out some sugar. "Here, Jet." He stroked her smooth, black neck. She nickered. Then she sniffed, and he felt her warm breath on his hand. Suddenly, with one swift movement of her head, Jet reached for the sugar.

"Good girl," said Benjy softly.

As the horse balanced on three legs and munched the sugar, Jim examined the cast and her upper leg. When he was finished, he motioned Benjy into the aisle and closed the stall door.

"I like the way you handled the mare," Jim said.

Benjy was so proud, his chest hurt.

"You're learning. You'll be a fine horseman."

Benjy smiled at Sherri. She smiled back.

The barn door swung open, and Linda entered. "Hi gang," she said. "How's Jet?"

"Holding her own," Jim answered. He turned to Benjy. "I'll be back in an hour for your lesson. Have Socks saddled. Okay?"

"Sure." The word sounded matter-of-fact, but Benjy could barely get it past his lips. For him, his first riding lesson would be the most exciting event since he'd arrived at Lakeside Farm.

Jim asked Linda, "Are you going to work Trouble Seeker this morning?"

"Yes. He should be ready today. He was much too upset yesterday to try anything."

"Well, good luck. See you later."

Sherri said, "Trouble Seeker is all set, Mom. He didn't want to stand still while I tacked him up."

"It's time to make Trouble forget that he was once a racehorse," Linda said.

"How do you do that, Linda?" asked Benjy.

"By slowing him down. And that's the exact opposite of what a jockey did."

"How long do you think it'll take to retrain him?" Sherri asked her mother.

Linda was thoughtful. "Oh, four, maybe five weeks. Trouble has a mind of his own. And a very tender mouth. That's why I'm using a rubber bit."

When Linda led the chestnut Thoroughbred toward the outdoor arena, his feet danced. He snorted as he passed Benjy and thrust his nose at Benjy's cap. Benjy jerked his head back, and the cap fell off. The horse whinnied and Benjy laughed. "Trouble, you're something else! If you don't knock off my cap, you make *me* do it."

Arcaro flew over and settled on the fence nearby. It seemed as if the bird was becoming attached to Trouble Seeker. In the barn, the crow perched in the hayloft over Trouble's stall. He hovered around the Thoroughbred in the pasture. Now he perched quietly on the fence rail and watched as Trouble Seeker tossed his head and pawed the ground.

Benjy stood out of the way and watched.

The horse seemed to know something was going to happen. Sweat covered Trouble's flanks as Linda dropped the stirrups, making them much longer than a jockey's. There was no meanness in

Trouble's eyes, Benjy thought, but the horse looked scared.

While Linda spoke softly to Trouble Seeker to calm him, Sherri told Benjy Trouble's story. "He had a broken bone in his foot, so they put a steel bar across the sole for support," she explained. "Trouble raced that way until the pain was too much. When he couldn't race any more, Dad bought him."

"Jim told me they were going to destroy him," Benjy said.

"Right. But Dad wouldn't let them. He figured there was some reason for all the pain. When our blacksmith peeled slivers of Trouble's hoof, he found a huge sore under the middle of the sole."

"Poor Trouble Seeker."

"Dad didn't give up. He put medicine in Trouble's hoof and told the blacksmith to make a special leather pad to cover the sole. Then he nailed a shoe on it. They removed the pad and put more medicine on every month for six months."

"Did it hurt him a lot?"

Sherri nodded. "He limped for a long time. But now the infection is all cleared up."

"And today, Trouble Seeker the racehorse becomes Trouble Seeker the pleasure horse."

"He's got a long way to go," laughed Sherri. "Look, Mom is ready."

Linda swung into the saddle with one easy motion. Just as she settled in the seat, Trouble stood up on his hind legs and reared. He almost went over backward, taking Linda with him.

Benjy held his breath. He loved Trouble Seeker, but he didn't envy Linda riding him. He realized how reckless he had been yesterday when he had tried to ride that horse.

Linda pressed forward against the horse's withers with all her strength. Trouble Seeker came down. But as soon as his forelegs touched the ground he took a mighty leap forward and galloped out across the yard.

Benjy gasped. Was Trouble Seeker going to run away with Linda, too?

Sherri exclaimed, "That horse can really go!"

Trouble Seeker galloped at full speed toward the opposite end of the arena. The wind gusted around the barn, whipping his chestnut mane and tail. He looked like the painting of a beautiful wild horse hanging in Benjy's school library.

"Can we do something?" Benjy asked Sherri.

"No. If we run after them, Trouble will be uncontrollable. Mom must manage to slow him down and turn him."

"Will she do it?"

Sherri bit her lip. "She's got to."

Benjy felt the same kind of lump in his throat

he'd had yesterday when he tried to yell for help. He was sure Linda would be crushed against the fence. He prayed that she would be able to slow Trouble Seeker in time to escape.

The racehorse neared the end of the arena. Swinging herself over in the saddle, Linda leaned with her entire body against the Thoroughbred's inner side. Using her hands and knees, she turned the horse. Trouble was so near the fence that his hoof scraped it.

Benjy heaved a sigh of relief. "Man, was that ever close!"

Sherri yelled, "Good going, Mom!"

Trouble Seeker continued racing along the fence. But soon his speed slackened, and Linda pulled him down to a slow canter. She was breathing hard now as she slowed Trouble to a trot, then a walk, and brought him to the gate where Sherri and Benjy stood.

"Wow!" said Sherri. "That was some ride!"

Linda's face shone with sweat. She leaned down and stroked the chestnut's foam-covered neck. "I'm glad it's over."

Trouble's nostrils quivered. His flanks heaved in and out. But he stood quietly.

Linda dismounted. "Trouble Seeker is a long way from a pleasure horse, but it's a start."

Arcaro swooped down from a tree. He hovered

42

around Trouble Seeker, cawing loudly. Trouble turned his head and nickered.

Benjy laughed. "These two like each other."

Sherri and Benjy hosed, sponged, and wiped Trouble Seeker clean. Then they walked him dry in the yard.

"Caw! Caw!" Arcaro circled the horse.

"Arcaro, is Trouble Seeker your friend?" Benjy asked his crow. "Say, 'you bet!'" coaxed Benjy.

Sherri watched the crow with an expectant look on her face. Arcaro fluttered his wings, dipped a few times like an airplane coming in for a landing, and lit on Trouble Seeker's back.

"Caw! Caw!"

Trouble Seeker turned his head. Benjy gasped, fearing what the Thoroughbred would do. But Trouble only gave a loud nicker.

"Look at that!" Sherri laughed.

Benjy slapped his thigh. "I knew those two were getting to be friends!"

Their sides ached from laughter as Benjy and Sherri watched the black crow hop up and down the racehorse's back, cawing loudly. Sherri finally looked at her watch.

"Hey, it's almost time for your lesson, Benjy. Let's put Trouble in his stall and tack up Socks."

Sherri tethered the palomino pony in the crossties. As Benjy went into the tack room there was a sudden gust of wind, and the barn door slammed.

Trouble Seeker snorted and pawed his stall, roughing up the bedding. But Socks, in the aisle, didn't blink an eye.

Sherri worked the currycomb over Socks's coat. "Nothing bothers you, does it, Socks?" She turned to Benjy. "He's our most dependable horse."

Benjy felt good about that. He pulled the pony's head toward him and brushed his white forelock.

"He's fat, too," Sherri added. "He's an easy keeper. He eats, sleeps, and does his job with beginning riders. He's okay."

The door slammed again and Paul entered. Without saying a word to Benjy or Sherri, he went over to Cherokee's stall. Patting the old horse's neck, he said, "Hi, fella. Dad wants you to get some exercise. Out you go."

Paul slid open old Cherokee's door and attached a lead chain to his halter. He led the pinto down the aisle past Socks. When he opened the outer door, a gust of wind tore through the barn.

Cherokee looked out and sniffed. Then he made a swift turn and headed back to his stall.

"Cherokee won't go out," Paul said. "Guess there's too much wind."

"Say, Paul," said Benjy, "do you think he's okay? He didn't finish his feed."

Paul frowned. "He always eats everything."

"Maybe Dr. Egel can look at Cherokee when he gives Jet her shots," suggested Benjy.

"For once you came up with a good idea, superstar."

Benjy's fist clenched around the polishing brush. Paul knew how to get to him, he thought. Superstar!

"I won't be here tomorrow morning," Paul went on. "I've got to get two horses ready. Lori and Sara are having early lessons. If I don't see the doc, be sure and tell him to look at Cherokee."

Benjy said, "Okay."

"And don't play around with your dumb crow and forget!" A blast of warm wind hit the aisle again, and Paul left the barn.

As Sherri combed Socks's white mane, she shook her head. "I can't understand what's happened to Paul."

I'm what's happened to Paul, Benjy thought.

Then Sherri said, "I know Paul misses Danny. They were best friends for three years. But he doesn't have to take it out on you."

Benjy couldn't worry about Paul now. It was time for his riding lesson. He had to concentrate and do everything right. It was the first step toward being a jockey, like Danny.

5
A Hard Riding Lesson

JIM AND BENJY led Socks to the small arena, and Sherri climbed the fence to watch the lesson. Arcaro perched on the fence rail.

Jim began by reviewing what Sherri had already taught Benjy about the saddle, bridle, and the parts of the horse. Benjy was impatient. When would he ride Socks?

There was a noise at the rail. Benjy turned and saw Mara Salamon climb up beside Sherri. The knees of her jeans were stained with mud from sneaking under the fence.

Finally Jim said, "Well, so much for the basics. Now walk to Socks's left side and talk to him."

Benjy's heart began to beat faster. Any minute now he'd be riding. "Hi, Socks," he said softly.

Socks swiveled his head and looked at Benjy. Then he flicked his tail at a fly.

"Okay," said Jim. "Socks knows you're there. Now check his saddle and bridle. Is the left stirrup long enough for you to get your toe in?"

Benjy nodded.

"Horses aren't as smart as dogs. They don't know how to think, but they have terrific memories. They remember things and form habits. Bad habits are hard to break."

Benjy wished that Jim would finish talking. He couldn't wait to ride.

But Jim went on. "If you don't ride properly, the horse can get the upper hand. You've got to make him understand and obey your signals."

Benjy remembered how Trouble Seeker had obeyed Linda. But when he had ridden the Thoroughbred, it had been a disaster.

"So if you want to be a good rider," continued Jim, "talk to Socks with your hands and legs, your voice, and the shifting of your weight. These are called your aids. I know you're anxious to get on the horse, but I don't want to hurry. We've got all summer to teach you to ride."

It won't take that long, thought Benjy. Not if I'm a natural.

"Okay," said Jim. "Ready to mount?"

Benjy was so anxious that he tripped over his boots and fell.

"Relax," Jim said, waiting for him to get to his

feet. "There are many ways to get on a horse. This is my way. Take your reins in your left hand and put them on the horse's neck, just in front of the saddle. Stand closer. Good!"

Benjy held the stirrup with his right hand. Then he reached up and awkwardly pushed his foot into the stirrup.

"You're digging Socks with your toe," said Jim.

Benjy did it again, more carefully. When Jim approved, he swung his right leg over Socks's rump and dropped into the saddle with a clump.

"Ouch!" exclaimed Jim. "How would you like ninety pounds of boy dropped on your back? Again!"

Sherri and Mara had left the arena. Benjy didn't blame them. This lesson would be boring to watch. He hadn't even walked the horse yet.

Socks was very patient while Benjy dismounted and mounted again. Benjy thought of Trouble Seeker's reaction when he had plopped on his back. Now Benjy knew that a good rider eased into the saddle.

Finally Jim allowed Benjy to remain in the seat. "Let your elbows hang naturally, but keep them close to your sides," he directed. "Put your heels down and toes up in the stirrups. Your calves must have contact with the horse's sides. I don't want to see daylight between your knees and the saddle."

It wasn't easy for Benjy. Whenever he thought that he had the perfect sitting position, Jim corrected him. "Elbows in! Relax your shoulders! No! Your knees are too far from the saddle! I can still see daylight between your knee and the saddle!" Jim wiped his forehead.

Did Danny take this long to catch on? Benjy asked himself.

At last Jim let Benjy walk Socks. "Remember, this horse is trained to understand your signals," Jim said. "Make light contact with his mouth through the reins. Tell him what to do. When he does it, stop signalling."

When Socks started off, Benjy's hands were so wet they stuck to the reins. Socks walked slowly toward Jim. Then the horse thrust his neck out and made a turn. Benjy was caught off balance. He became confused, lost the stirrup, and slid along the side of the saddle. Jim caught him before he fell and pushed him upright.

Jim looked thoughtful. "You need balance exercises. Keep your left hand on the reins. Reach forward and pat Socks behind the ears. Bring your arm in a circle over your head. Extend it back and pat his rump. Now, lean down and touch your toe without lifting your foot."

Benjy did the exercises over and over. He knew now it would take work to become a jockey.

At last Jim said, "Well, that's it for today, Benjy. I've thrown an awful lot at you. You've got a problem with balance."

Benjy felt the muscles in his cheeks tighten. Would Jim give up working with him?

"Do you know where the small indoor ring is?"

Benjy nodded.

"Practice the balancing exercises out there on Socks, twice a day. Then walk him around the ring when you catch on to the correct sitting position. I'll get Sherri to work with you. Do a few body exercises, too. Lie back in the saddle, cross your arms on your chest, and pretend to nap. Then see if you can sit up without using your hands."

Benjy was almost afraid to ask, "Will you give me another lesson?"

"In a few days. There'll be two each week."

Happy that Jim would still teach him, Benjy dismounted. He didn't have to ask if he were a natural. He thought back to this morning with Jet when Jim had said, "You're learning. You'll be a fine horseman." What would Jim say now?

Jim must have read his thoughts. "You can still be a fine horseman, Benjy," he said. "But a fine horseman isn't always a fine rider."

Benjy pondered Jim's statement while he walked Socks to the barn. *"But a jockey must be a fine rider!"* he said aloud as he reached for the crossties in the aisle. He resolved to practice until he had perfect balance.

Arcaro hopped on Benjy's shoulder and pecked at the stripes on his shirt. Then he screeched, "Ben-nn-njy! Ben-nn-njy! Six o'clock!"

"Hi, Arcaro," Benjy said, smiling at his crow

Trouble Seeker poked his head out to see what was going on. He neighed, starting a chorus of neighs from the other horses. Then in one quick movement, the mischievious horse again shoved Benjy's cap off with his nose.

Before Benjy could retrieve it, Arcaro swooped down. Then he disappeared into the hayloft, the faded red cap in his beak.

"Hey!" Benjy shouted. "My cap! Are you two working together?"

Mara came into the barn. "Sherri here?"

Benjy said, "Nobody's here but me."

"Who were you yelling at?"

"My crow, Arcaro. He stole my cap." Benjy removed Socks's bridle and buckled on his halter.

"I saw Arcaro on the fence during your riding lesson. He's cute."

At the mention of his riding lesson, Benjy felt his face flush.

"Where is Arcaro now?"

"Up there." The crow was perched on a bale of hay, the red cap dangling from his beak.

"Sherri says that Arcaro can talk, but she's never heard him. Can I?"

Benjy dipped Socks's bridle in the water bucket and wiped the bit with a towel. "He won't speak when there're a lot of people around."

"I'm not a lot of people."

Benjy said, "Well ... okay. Let's try." He put his finger over his lips. "Be very quiet. Arcaro doesn't like noise."

"I'll get in the corner. He won't even notice me."

"Arcaro! Arcaro!" called Benjy.

The crow opened his beak to answer, "Caw! Caw!" Benjy's cap dropped.

"Thanks, Arcaro." Benjy put on his cap and held out his hand. "Come here, boy."

Arcaro flew around the cobwebbed ceiling

beams. Then he lit on Benjy's outstretched palm.

"Are you a good boy?" Benjy asked.

The crow's large eyes darted around the barn lingering on Mara. "Caw! Caw!"

Mara pressed her back into the corner.

Arcaro fluttered his wings as if he were about to take off. But instead he just hopped up and down on Benjy's hand.

Benjy asked again, "Are you a good boy?"

"You bet!" Arcaro squawked.

Mara's eyes danced. "Make him say more."

"Call Benjy! Benn-nn-njy! Ben-nn-njy!"

Arcaro screeched, "Ben-nn-njy! Six o'clock!"

Mara giggled. "That crow is really something!"

Arcaro turned his head, and his big black eyes stared at Mara. Benjy thought he'd surely fly away, but Arcaro seemed to enjoy performing for Mara.

"Ben-nn-njy! You bet!" squawked the crow.

"Tell him to say, 'Mara.'"

"I'll try. Sometimes if I repeat a word over and over, he'll say it. That's how I taught him the other things." Benjy stroked his pet. "C'mon Arcaro, say, 'Mara. Mara. Mara.'"

But Arcaro took off for Trouble Seeker's stall. The interview was over.

Mara heaved a sigh. "Benjy, you're so lucky! You've got Arcaro and all these horses." She swept her arm to take in the entire barn. "And riding lessons. I'd give *anything* for riding lessons!"

"Guess your mother won't let you take them."

Mara nodded glumly. "Once when Mom was about sixteen, she went riding. The cinch broke underneath the horse, and she fell off, saddle and all. She broke her arm, and she's deathly afraid that something bad will happen to me."

"Suppose your mother didn't know about the lessons?"

Mara ran her fingers through her short, blonde hair. "No way. I've begged Jim and Linda to teach me. I saved my allowance for a whole year to pay. They say I'm welcome to come here, but they won't even let me touch a horse."

"What about Sherri?"

"She taught me the parts of a horse and about the equipment, but that's all."

Benjy felt sorry for Mara. She looked so unhappy. He wished he could help her. She'd helped him when he'd landed in her mother's rose garden. "I think you're a brave girl to come here."

"Brave! I love horses. I wish I could ride Socks. Listen, Benjy, don't take off Socks's saddle. Please let me ride him. Just once," Mara begged.

"I don't know," answered Benjy.

"Nobody's around. We can take him to the small indoor ring out back. Only for a few minutes. Please!"

Benjy said, "Well—okay. Just this once. I'll put Socks's bridle on again."

"Benjy! Would you? That's super!"

By the time Benjy had the bridle on, he was having second thoughts about letting Mara ride. Why do I always act first and think later? he asked himself. Linda had told him never to ride without permission. But, he rationalized, Jim had given him permission to use Socks. He hoped nothing would go wrong this time. Anyway, he couldn't disappoint Mara now.

Socks walked obediently to the indoor ring.

"Okay," Benjy said. "Now go over to his left side and tell Socks you're there."

Her eyes shining, Mara said, "Hi, Socks. It's me, Mara. I'm going to ride." She checked the stirrups according to Benjy's instructions. Then, like a graceful dancer, she eased her body into the saddle.

"Look who's riding a horse!" she cried.

Benjy stared. Mara sat tall in the seat, shoulders back, eyes straight ahead, heels down. There was no daylight between her knees and the saddle. Her body was in perfect alignment.

"Well?" Mara asked. "What kind of exercises should I do?"

Mara didn't need balancing exercises. Or any other kind of exercises.

She was a natural.

6
At the Racetrack

DURING THE NEXT FEW WEEKS Benjy grew used to the routine at Lakeside. He loved getting up early and tending the horses. His letters to his parents reported Jet's progress, and Jim's compliments on his care of the sick horse.

Paul seemed to leave Benjy alone, and Benjy was glad. He had plenty of other things to think about. Although he hadn't planned on Mara riding Socks again, it worked out that way. After every lesson with Jim, Benjy brought the horse to the indoor ring and met Mara there. She caught on quickly to what Benjy had been taught. But he had to practice over and over.

Benjy learned how to signal Socks, how to take up a trot from a walk, and how to sit a slow trot. "Drop your feet out of the stirrups," Jim had said.

"Now shift your weight so that you're almost upright. The trick is to relax while keeping the correct leg and body position."

Working on the slow trot improved the way Benjy sat in the saddle. But when Jim tried to teach him to post a full trot, Benjy bounced awkwardly.

Sherri worked with Benjy in the back ring two or three times a week. Benjy tried his best to master posting the full trot, but he didn't make much progress. After a month of extra practice, Sherri was exasperated.

"Benjy, it's time you caught on to posting," she said one afternoon. "Why can't you get the rhythm? Start over."

When Benjy mounted Socks, Sherri said, "Do this. It's really simple. Sit in the saddle when Socks's foreleg touches the ground. Then rise in the stirrups, just a few inches above the saddle when the leg is in the air."

Benjy tried, but still he went bump, bump, bump.

"Lean forward a little, lift up, then ease yourself back into the saddle. Your timing is wrong," Sherri explained patiently.

Benjy tried again. Bump, bump.

"No!" cried Sherri. She tossed her head vigorously, making his pigtails whirl about her face. "Now I see it, you're using your muscles to raise you. Don't do it. Let Socks do the work."

Benjy began posting again.

"Feel the rhythm? Up, down. Up, down." Sherri clapped her hands in time with the words.

Benjy caught on. He began to move with the beat of her hands.

"That's it!" exlaimed Sherri.

Benjy didn't want to lose the rhythm. He made up a rhyme. "Up, down. Up, down. Yankee Doodle came to town." He said it again and again.

Sherri sighed. "You finally got it."

Benjy felt wonderful after his successful practice session with Sherri. He whistled "Yankee Doodle" loudly as he led Socks to the stall area.

As he arrived, Dr. Egel was leaving Jet's stall.

"How is she?" Benjy asked the veterinarian.

"Coming along nicely. I hope to take the cast off in a couple of weeks. When we x-ray the leg, we'll know for sure. You've done a good job, son. She seems quite comfortable."

"She's a game girl," Benjy said. "And Cherokee?"

The doctor frowned. "I've tried vitamins and tonic, but the horse is old and full of arthritis ..." He shook his head.

Cherokee rarely finished his grain now, even when Benjy fed him sweet feed and molasses. And although Paul tempted his old pony with daily treats of carrots and sugar, Cherokee hardly touched them. He left his stall only on mild days when the wind was calm. Then he'd stand out in the pasture and doze.

As Benjy walked to the door with Dr. Egel, he saw Lori Oostdyke. She was leading her horse, Magic. "Benjy, I want to talk to you," she said.

When he came out, Sara Morris and Carmen Withrow were in the yard with Lori. "Listen, Benjy," Lori said, "I'm in charge of Lakeside Farm's entry in the parade. Want to be in it?"

"What parade?"

"Braeburn Homecoming—the Labor Day parade. The group with the most creative float or marching unit wins a hundred-dollar contribution to their favorite charity. There'll be judges and everything."

Carmen said, "Last year the Lakeside riders dressed as Teddy Roosevelt's Rough Riders. We won honorable mention."

"We need something really super," said Lori. "So we can win the money for the Association for Equine Research. Any ideas, Benjy?"

Benjy had seen many parades in Chicago. "I like circus parades best," he said. "Maybe Lakeside can represent a circus."

"I like that!" exclaimed Lori. "Magic and I can carry the flags and lead the march."

Sara was enthusiastic, too. "I've got a pink ballet costume. I'll be an aerial trapeze performer."

"I'll ride Julep bareback," offered Carmen. "Maybe I can learn some tricks."

"If Jim lets me use Socks, I can be a clown!" Benjy said.

Lori said, "Great! Sherri and Paul are in the parade, and Anne Fritzinger and some other kids. I'll call a meeting soon."

That afternoon Benjy met Jim in the yard and asked for permission to ride in the parade.

Jim nodded. "You should be able to handle Socks by then."

Was there any doubt in Jim's mind? Labor Day was almost six weeks away! Benjy was going to question him, but Jim changed the subject. "Danny Hoffman is riding in the fifth race at Arlington today, Benjy. How'd you like to meet him and see what the backstretch is like?"

"Man, would I!" Benjy was eager to visit the racetrack where he hoped to work some day. And he couldn't wait to meet Danny.

Jim said, "Danny's come a long way in three years. He took lessons on Socks, just like you. Then he rode one of our older Thoroughbreds. In about a year, he was able to work a young racehorse."

Benjy wondered if he would advance the way

Danny had. "Then did Danny become a jockey?"

"Not yet. He still had a lot to learn. He breezed horses at the track for me in the mornings."

Benjy was puzzled.

"That means working a horse the way a jockey does in a race," Jim explained. "Danny practiced for a long time, sitting in the saddle the way a jockey does, breaking from the starting gate, leaning into turns, timing and rating."

"Rating?"

"That's holding back a horse in a race until it's time to make a run for the finish line."

"Then Danny became a jockey?"

"Yes. He got his license and rode races on small tracks for experience. This is his first season at a big track like Arlington. He's still a bug."

"What's a bug?"

"An apprentice rider. An apprentice and his equipment can weigh less than a regular jockey. The lighter the load, the better the chance of winning, so a bug has a chance racing against experienced jockeys. Well, Benjy, I've got to get back to the track. Check with Linda. She and the kids are going over to Arlington after lunch."

That afternoon, when Linda's blue pickup arrived at Arlington Park Race Track, Benjy couldn't wait to jump out. Linda handed her pass to the track policeman. Benjy noticed an

62

ambulance parked at the gate as they went in.

The backstretch was a lively place. Benjy wrinkled his nose at the pungent odors of liniment, boot polish, and manure. Stable hands mucked stalls and fed horses amid loud neighs, nickers, and the clatter of horse hooves.

Nearby, a groom knelt and wrapped wide bands of cotton around a Thoroughbred's slender legs.

As they went through the stall area, Sherri pointed to a slim girl in jeans and T-shirt slowly walking a horse. "There's a hot-walker. She's walking a horse to cool him off after a race."

Paul said, "Dad's over there."

Jim stood near a line of flapping laundry. A sign on the stall said "Louis Kahnweiler Stables." Mr. Kahnweiler owned the racehorses that Jim trained.

When a Thoroughbred stuck out his head and nickered, Benjy wondered how temperamental racehorses endured all the noise.

Jim called, "Hi, family! We've got a wad of cotton in the young filly's ears to keep out the racket. Want some?" He chuckled.

So that's what they do, Benjy thought.

Jim said, "The young filly isn't used to the noise yet, but Calico Kate thrives on commotion. For her, it's like post time with the band playing, the crowd yelling..."

Calico Kate was the four-year-old mare that

Danny was riding in the fifth race. Danny had finished third with her last week. She was one of two favorites in today's race. The sleek brown Thoroughbred with alert, wide-set eyes pranced on her muscular white-stockinged legs. Head high, Calico Kate swelled her chest, and her nostrils trembled.

Linda patted the mare's arched neck. "She's feeling good."

"Where's Danny?" Benjy asked Jim.

"In the jockeys' quarters underneath the bandstand. We're not allowed to go there now. Too close to post time."

"Danny's probably playing cards," Paul said, chuckling.

Benjy knew he wouldn't be relaxed enough to play cards before a race. He'd be chewing his nails.

A young man carried Calico Kate's tack to the saddling enclosure in the paddock. She was led into the small, roofed shed with a number four over it. Four was the post position that Danny had drawn for the race.

Mr. Kahnweiler, Calico Kate's owner, waited in the paddock. He talked to Jim.

Jim stood on the horse's left side. He and the groom saddled her. "Hold the mare while I adjust the cinch," Jim told the groom. Then he checked her overgirth, another strap that helped to hold the

64

saddle in place. When the straps were right, Jim examined Calico Kate's feet, legs, and chest. "She's in fine shape," he said.

Paul said, "Here's Danny." He sounded as if he was announcing a Kentucky Derby winner.

Danny shook hands with Mr. Kahnweiler. The jockey was slim and about Benjy's height. His green eyes matched the emerald and white diamond-patterned silks of the Kahnweiler Stables. He had on shiny black boots and a white cap with goggles pushed above the visor. An elastic band held a large white number four near the shoulder of his right arm.

Danny ignored Sherri and turned to Paul. "How's it going?" he asked.

Paul's gray eyes lit up with warmth that Benjy had never seen. "Great, Danny. Just great."

"Meet Benjy Tennen, our new boy," said Jim.

"Hi," said Danny.

"I've heard a lot about you," Benjy said.

Danny smiled, and his eyes looked even greener than before.

Calico Kate pawed the ground anxiously. Her white stockings were filmed with gray dust. She threw her head, and the well-combed mane fell tousled about her neck.

Outside the stall, a girl on a palomino stable pony waited to lead the racehorse to the post.

Seeing the palomino standing patiently reminded Benjy that Cherokee and Socks had once been lead ponies at the racetrack.

The paddock judge called, "Riders up!" A quiver of excitement streaked up Benjy's spine. Someday, Jim would be lifting Benjy into the saddle as he was doing now with Danny—so Benjy hoped.

Jim reviewed his instructions. "Remember, Ginger is the horse to beat. Gil Passolas, her jockey, is plenty tough. He wants to win, and he's one of the best. Good luck!"

Sherri told Benjy, "Gil Passolas is the top apprentice jockey at the track this season. He has twenty-eight wins."

Paul said, "You'll beat 'em Danny!"

Danny nodded and patted Calico Kate's neck. Carrying only one hundred and ten pounds, he looked small and pale on the tall, brown horse. But he sat in the saddle easy and relaxed. He picked up the reins, and Calico Kate circled the paddock. Head high, the spirited racehorse had an eager, graceful walk. Benjy wished that he were up there in the saddle.

A red-coated bugler standing in the middle of the track blew the call to the post. It was the first time Benjy had heard the thrilling notes, and he shivered in anticipation.

Over the track loudspeaker the announcer said, "Nine horses will be going to the post, ladies and gentlemen." Then he gave the names and racing backgrounds of the horses in the race.

Led by the palomino pony, Calico Kate joined the other Thoroughbreds walking single file onto the track. The excitable high-steppers nudged and pushed against their lead ponies, while the jockeys' bright silks shimmered in the afternoon sun.

Benjy and the Spears stood on the steps next to the winner's circle to watch the race. Linda gave Benjy a pair of binoculars. He quickly found Danny and Calico Kate. Danny's green and white clad body never moved out of the saddle. Ginger seemed edgy and anxious. Gil Passolas tried to restrain the chestnut mare.

The grandstands were jammed with tense people waiting for the race to begin.

Linda pointed out the gate on the far side of the track where the horses would start. "This race is a mile long," she said.

Jim explained, "The mile is marked off in furlongs. A furlong is one-eighth of a mile. There'll be four furlongs to the turn, two more going around it, and then two furlongs to the finish wire."

"The purse is $5,000," Sherri said.

"And Danny's going to win," said Paul.

"He's got a darn good chance," Jim said. "Most of the jockeys in this race are bugs, but Danny's won more races."

Peering through the binoculars, Benjy watched the jockeys, with whips in their hands, ride slowly toward the gate.

The announcer said, "The horses have reached the starting gate."

"Close 'em up," ordered the starter. The front latches were locked. Benjy saw the horses milling behind the gate, waiting to be led into the narrow, padded stalls by the assistant starters. Gil Passolas was standing in the stirrups. Danny looked calm, almost grim, waiting his turn. Then he pulled the goggles over his eyes, and Calico Kate was steered into number four starting stall. Benjy noticed that a woman jockey was in number five.

The announcer said, "The horses are at the post!"

Danny crouched low over his mount. His legs were raised at a sharp angle. Benjy couldn't see his face because it was hidden against Calico Kate.

The crowd was quiet now. Benjy held his breath as the starter on the elevated stand pressed the button. A bell shrilled, and the stall doors flew open. The loudspeaker crackled, and the announcer shouted, "They're off!"

68

7
Danny Fights to the Finish

BENJY LEANED FORWARD and cheered. "Go! Go!"

"C'mon, Danny!" yelled Paul. Turning to Benjy, he said, "Now you'll see a real jockey, superstar."

When the stall doors opened, horses leaped out in a tremendous rush. Jockeys' heads and shoulders seemed to be jammed together, and there was frantic pushing and pounding. Although Benjy's binoculars were trained on the starting gate, he couldn't find Danny. He was somewhere in the middle of the pack, a greenish blur among all the jockeys' colored silks.

Benjy shouted to Jim. "Look, the jockeys are all shoved together. That fellow is pinched against the fence."

"Racing is rough business," Jim said. "But jockeys learn to handle it. Danny will pull out of the pack before the turn." His words were confident, but he sounded worried.

Hooves pounded the turf as the horses swept down the track. Benjy finally found Danny in the tangled mass. He was hunched over Calico Kate, driving his heels into the horse's sides. He leaned into her to guide her toward a small open space, but a black horse galloped up and beat him to it. Benjy could barely make out Calico Kate's head as she fell back into the pack. He lost horse and rider in a maze of legs, tails, and bobbing heads.

Benjy's eyes shifted to the two horses running ahead of the rest. The favorite, Ginger, ridden by Gil Passolas, was in the lead along the rail. In second position, Barbara Stein's horse, Cinappa, challenged the pacesetter. Heading toward the turn Ginger and Cinappa ate up ground.

Benjy hoped that Danny would break out of the pack and move up to challenge Ginger and Cinappa. Calico Kate tried to find an opening, but she was blocked.

Then Danny put on a sudden burst of speed. Although there was very little room, he urged his mount toward a narrow opening between two outside horses.

Linda let out a shout. "Danny's trying to squeeze through!"

Leaning forward in his saddle, Danny guided

Calico Kate. Responding to his hands, his horse plunged in, brushing the bodies of the two horses on the outside and barely avoiding a collision. The horses pulled apart and Calico Kate raced through.

"Danny did it!" cried Sherri.

Paul said, "Now watch him go!"

The announcer's voice came over the loudspeaker. "At the turn—Ginger on top by a head, Cinappa running second, Calico Kate coming up fast on the outside. Dodson is running fourth, Profit fifth, with Lucky Buck and Apache neck

and neck on the rail. Angel eighth by half a length, and Duke is trailing."

Calico Kate stretched her long legs and pounded the turf, striving to catch the leaders. But they thundered ahead, setting a furious pace.

Danny made the turn just as Ginger and Cinappa entered the homestretch. The two horses were staying together. Only two more furlongs, a quarter of a mile to go! Would he catch them?

The crowd rose. They roared as Calico Kate came off the turn and picked up speed. Danny was closing the gap!

Paul shouted, "Atta boy, Danny!"

Ginger, the front runner, wobbled and slackened her pace. Gil Passolas whipped his horse frantically, but Cinappa overtook Ginger. Barbara Stein had a clear path to the finish wire.

"Now, Danny! Now!" shouted Jim.

"Let 'er go!" Linda urged.

It was time for Danny to race for the wire in a come-from-behind finish.

Using hands and feet to urge his horse on, Danny moved up even with Gil Passolas. Then smoothly passing his whip from his right hand to his left, he lashed his mount. It was the signal for Calico Kate to make her drive down the outside to the wire. She quickly passed the tiring Ginger and raced for the lead.

Barbara Stein used her whip, too, and burst for the finish line.

The crowd yelled as the two jockeys fought for the lead. Every inch counted. First one head bobbed forward, then the other. Suddenly Cinappa misstepped and lost ground to Calico Kate.

"Barbara's finished!" cried Paul, his voice high pitched with excitement.

But Barbara Stein didn't give up. She switched her whip smoothly from hand to hand and whipped her mount, driving him until Cinappa was again side by side with Calico Kate.

"The race isn't over yet!" Paul yelled.

"That Barbara can ride!" said Sherri.

Danny's face was buried against Calico Kate's neck. She was running wide open now, taking gigantic strides. Then with concentrated speed, she stretched out, very low. Her head inched in front of Cinappa, and she swept under the finish wire.

Winner by a nose!

The crowd whistled, stamped, and cheered. They had seen a spectacular race. Benjy pounded Paul's back, and Sherri jumped up and down. Linda and Jim hugged each other.

The official standings appeared on the scoreboard. The announcer called out, "Ladies and gentlemen, in the fifth race, the winner by a nose, Calico Kate. Second place Cinappa, and Ginger third."

Jogging into the winner's circle, Danny flashed a triumphant smile. He patted Calico Kate's neck, lathered with foam. Mr. Kahnweiler beamed as he posed with his winning horse and jockey for a newspaper photographer. The Spears and Benjy, too, had several pictures taken with Calico Kate and Danny.

How Benjy envied Danny! On the way home he relived the race again and again in his mind. He imagined himself astride Calico Kate, pounding toward the finish wire. He saw himself stepping into the winner's circle, surrounded by reporters.

When they arrived back at Lakeside, Benjy ran up to his room and took out Eddie Arcaro's book, *I Ride to Win!* Reading it again, he felt reassured that he had the right physical build to be a jockey. But when he came to the part that said a good riding seat and hands are the fundamentals of race riding, he frowned and bit his lip. Did he have those fundamentals? "I'll be a jockey, or else!" he said aloud.

Or else, what? For the first time, Benjy allowed himself to think of failure. "Or I'll go home, play baseball, and forget about horses forever!"

During the following week, Jim began teaching

Benjy the canter. He explained, "To take up the canter you need good coordination of hand and leg aids." He showed Benjy how to put Socks on the left-and-right leads in order to turn him.

"When you ride the canter, don't move your head or the upper part of your body," Jim said. "All of the movement is in your hips."

There's a certain three-beat rhythm, thought Benjy, watching Jim.

Jim said, "Heels lower than toes. Don't grip too hard with your knees. Just keep light contact with the saddle. Sit on your sitting bones. Relax and go with the motion of the horse."

During one lesson Paul came up. He stood watching, arms folded across his chest.

Now I'll show Paul something, Benjy said to himself. He crouched over Socks the way Danny had hunched over Calico Kate racing down the backstretch. He signaled Socks to canter. But in the excitement of trying to be like Danny, Benjy lost the stirrups and control of his legs. He kicked his horse's sides again and again, urging him on. Around and around the small arena Socks went.

"Stop kicking that horse!" shouted Jim.

"Whoa!" Benjy cried in a muffled voice. His face was buried in the horse's mane. But Socks kept circling the arena, obeying the frantic leg signals hitting his ribs.

Then, dripping with sweat, Socks tired and stumbled. Benjy let go of the reins and slid over the horse's side to the ground. When Benjy fell, Socks stopped and stood quietly, his body heaving. Jim ran over.

Benjy got to his feet. "I'm okay." he told Jim.

Paul cried, "Hey, superstar, inspecting real estate again? You're on the ground more than you're on the horse." He sauntered off, laughing.

When Jim had made certain that Benjy and Socks were not hurt, he said, "Benjy, who told you to lean over that horse's neck and keep kicking him?"

"I couldn't help it," said Benjy. "I was so excited I couldn't make my legs and arms do what I wanted them to do."

"You've seen and heard the noise and excitement at the racetrack, Benjy. In a race, there's always that confusion plus the pressure to win. A jockey must be in control of himself and his horse. Think about it."

Benjy thought about what Jim had said all during dinner. He thought about it later that evening when he was in the laundry room with Arcaro. The crow was in a playful mood. He hopped from Benjy's right shoulder to his left, trying to get his attention.

"Six o'clock!" he cawed. He pecked at the checks

on Benjy's red shirt. Then he said, "It's Mara!"

Although Benjy had been saying "It's Mara" to the crow dozens of times a day for over a month, Arcaro had never repeated the phrase before.

"Caw! Caw! It's Mara!"

But Benjy was too upset to notice. "Good boy," he said absently, giving Arcaro a pat.

There's six more weeks to go, he thought as he sorted his underwear. How can I stick it out? Man, I sure looked forward to coming here. Told the guys in the club what a great jockey I'd be. Great? I'm the worst. I can't do anything that Danny does. I can't even control that dumb old Socks. And they only use him for beginners. How will I ever ride a racehorse?

Someone was coming. Arcaro heard the footsteps. He cawed loudly and flew out the door, as Sherri entered with a bag of laundry.

"Oh, hi, Sherri," Benjy said.

Sherri dumped out her clothes and began sorting them. "Dad told me what happened at your lesson."

"I'll never be a jockey."

Sherri raised her voice over the clang of the washing machine. "It takes time to be a rider. A long time."

"You don't have to keep saying that!"

Why was he taking his anger out on Sherri? She

was his friend. "Listen, Sherri, I'll tell you something. Promise you won't laugh?"

"Promise."

Benjy hesitated, swallowing. "Well ... the reason I did that this afternoon was because I was trying to be like Danny." He waited a moment. "Maybe I should go home."

"Home!" Sherri burst out. "Are you a quitter?"

Benjy didn't answer.

"Why on earth would you want to be like Danny?" Sherri asked.

Benjy thought about that. Could he explain to Sherri the way Paul had acted when he came to take Danny's place? Benjy flushed when he thought of how he'd boasted that he'd be as good or better than Danny. And now there was Jim's disappointment with him for not even being able to ride Socks.

Benjy lifted out the clean, wet clothes and put them into the dryer. Then he shrugged. "Because I want to be a good jockey."

The machine was filling with water again and Benjy threw in his jeans and some soap.

Sherri said, "You're trying to walk in Danny's footsteps and that's not easy."

"Well, Danny's great," mumbled Benjy.

"He's a good jockey. But there were lots of things that Danny couldn't or wouldn't do."

78

"Like what?"

"Well, he'd never even talk to me. He'd never have a bird for a pet. He wouldn't take care of a sick horse, and he couldn't stand the sight of blood."

Benjy's jaw dropped. "Honestly?"

"Danny has a one-track mind . . . racing!"

"But Paul won't let anybody take Danny's place. Especially me."

"Paul misses Danny because they were friends. And I think he's mad because Danny has outgrown him. Paul's trying to hold on to the friendship. But he can't any longer—Danny's in a whole new world."

Benjy was quiet, thinking about what Sherri had said.

"I'll bet that if I worked with you a few evenings, Benjy, the extra practice would help a lot."

"Sherri, would you?"

She nodded. "Let's tack up Socks right now."

Benjy tripped over the clothes basket and fell. Then he got up, laughed, and raced off to saddle Socks.

8
Cherokee
in the Thunderstorm

"TROUBLE SEEKER is really calming down," Linda said at breakfast a week later. "He's turned into an excellent pleasure horse."

Benjy was making pancakes. He poured the batter onto the hot griddle, looked up, and caught Linda's eye.

"But he still needs an experienced rider," she said. Benjy flipped the pancakes. He knew that Linda meant he wasn't to ride Trouble Seeker.

Paul asked, "Where's Dad?"

Linda drank her orange juice. "He'll be along."

"Dr. Egel stopped in to talk to him," Sherri said.

The kitchen door opened. Jim walked over to the percolator. "Morning, all," he said, as he poured a cup of coffee. "I just talked to Dr. Egel." Jim glanced at Paul and hesitated. "There's good news about Jet. Dr. Egel will take off her cast next Thursday."

"Great!" Benjy exclaimed.

"I hope the infection's gone," said Linda.

Paul broke in. "What did he say about Cherokee?"

Jim swallowed a mouthful of coffee. "The horse is old, Paul. And very tired."

"But he's happy in his stall."

"That's just it. Cherokee doesn't leave it. He's so weak, he can barely stand."

Paul said, "Maybe if we tried ..."

"We've tried everything. I'm sorry, Paul, but Dr. Egel thinks we should put Cherokee to sleep."

"No!" cried Paul.

Linda said gently, "It's cruel to make Cherokee suffer. He can't survive another winter."

Benjy brought a stack of pancakes to the table and sat down with the others. He felt sad because he'd grown fond of the old track pony. He understood how much Cherokee meant to Paul.

Paul stared at the pancakes. Then he pushed back his chair. "I'm not hungry," he said, and he left the room.

After a brief silence, Jim said, "These pancakes are delicious, Benjy." He made a joke about the blueberry syrup matching Linda's riding shirt. But nobody smiled.

The Spears didn't linger at the table, and Benjy was able to finish his kitchen cleanup quickly.

Mara had asked if she could come over and ride Socks. He enjoyed helping her, but he wasn't sure how Jim and Linda would feel if they knew what was going on. He hadn't talked to them yet about Mara's riding lessons. He knew that he should, but the right moment never seemed to come.

Benjy saddled Socks and arrived at the indoor ring just in time. Mara was sad when he told her about Cherokee.

"Maybe you can feed him a little extra at night," she suggested. "We did that with our dog, and it really helped."

"He doesn't have much appetite, but ..." Benjy thought he'd try a late night feeding and see if it made a difference. He looked at the arena clock, "Let's get going, Mara. We can work on leads."

Mara mounted Socks and picked up the reins. She was in control as she signaled him into a right lead. Sitting tall and relaxed in the saddle, Mara circled the ring.

Benjy called. "That's great, Mara." He sighed. "I wish I could ride like that."

There was a noise behind him. Benjy turned quickly and saw Sherri. He flushed. How long had she been standing there?

Sherri said, "You're good, Mara. I didn't know you'd been taking lessons."

Mara and Benjy exchanged guilty looks.

"I helped Mara ride," Benjy said.

"You!" exclaimed Sherri.

"When Jim gives me a lesson, I show Mara what I've learned. She practices with Socks."

Mara broke in. "Don't blame Benjy. I love horses so much! I begged him to help me."

"Well, you sure know how to handle a horse, Mara. I can't believe that Benjy taught you your leads and everything. Because he ..."

Because I can't ride like that, Benjy thought. "Mara is a natural," he interrupted. "I'll bet she could even handle a racehorse."

Sherri turned to Mara, "Does your mother know?"

"No."

"Oh, boy!" said Sherri. "Wait until she finds out."

Mara's voice shook. "She doesn't have to know."

Sherri appeared to be making a decision. "Well, I'll never blab to her, but I think you should tell my dad. He could have a problem with your mother because you've been riding here."

Benjy said, "We don't want Jim to get into trouble. We just thought ..."

Sherri said, "You didn't think."

Benjy bit his lip. "I'll tell Jim tonight."

It was warm and muggy when Benjy walked to the barn for the late afternoon feeding. A storm was coming, and the sky was as dark as his thoughts. Why had he gotten involved with Mara when he knew that he shouldn't have? And this time it meant real trouble with Mara's mother. Jim had every right to tell him to pack his bags.

It was hot in the barn. Benjy took off his cap and wiped his forehead with the back of his hand. He hoped it would rain and cool off.

He heard wings flapping. Arcaro flew into the barn and dropped a seed he carried in his beak. Thrusting his neck forward in a pecking motion, he called, "Ben-nn-njy! Six o'clock!" Then he swooped down on Benjy's cap and picked off a shiny button pinned to it. The button said, "Fight smog, ride a horse." Arcaro flew up to the hayloft, cawing loudly.

"Arcaro!" Benjy called. "Come back." The crow swirled down and cried, "It's Mara!" Then he circled Trouble Seeker's stall and perched saucily between the Thoroughbred's ears. Benjy expected a violent reaction from Trouble Seeker, but the racehorse cocked his head as if to say, "Look at us!" He almost looked as if he were smiling.

Benjy laughed. "I wish I had a camera. No one will believe you two. Sitting on Trouble Seeker's back is one thing, old boy, but on his head... you're a real clown!"

Soon Arcaro darted into the hayloft again. Benjy

stood thinking about a night feeding for Cherokee and wondering how he would tell Jim about Mara's lessons. Trouble Seeker leaned over and pushed off his cap.

"Not again!" Benjy stooped to pick it up. "You caught me because my mind is on other things. But I'll catch you next time."

Benjy was still worrying about how to break the news to Jim about Mara's lessons when the dinner gong sounded. He was relieved to hear that Jim wouldn't be home until late. It might be better to tell him in the morning when he wasn't so tired.

Paul moped through dinner and went upstairs early. The rainstorm that had been threatening all day finally began. Linda, Sherri, and Benjy watched TV for a while, but the lightning made the screen flicker.

Benjy rubbed his eyes and decided to go to bed. He wondered if Paul was already asleep. Flashes of lightning made it easy to undress without turning on the lamp. Paul seemed to be sleeping so soundly that Benjy had no fear of waking him. There was a loud burst of thunder, but Paul didn't stir under the rumpled bedcovers.

Benjy crawled into bed, but he couldn't sleep. The angry thunder rumbled ominously and erupted in roaring bursts. How could Paul sleep through all the racket? Benjy thought about giving Cherokee extra food, but he hated to get up now and go out in the storm.

He tossed, flattening his pillow with his fist. Then he buried his head to shut out the thunder. But he couldn't get Cherokee out of his mind. Perhaps if he mixed some sweet feed with the oats that Cherokee used to like, the horse might be tempted to eat.

Benjy got out of bed, put on his jeans over his pajamas, and tiptoed downstairs in his bare feet. He pulled on his boots, grabbed a yellow slicker from behind the kitchen door, and ran to the barn.

A gust of wind blew him inside, and the door slammed behind him. The horses responded to the banging door with loud neighs and nickers. He headed toward Cherokee's stall. The sound of his boots clicking on the wooden floor was muffled by the pelting rain and the thunder which was now directly overhead. Benjy smelled the horses' warm, damp, bodies.

Cherokee's door was wide open! The old horse was lying on his belly with his feet tucked under him. Someone knelt beside him, talking in soothing tones. It was Paul. No wonder Benjy hadn't seen him move under the lumpy bed-clothes. He'd been here all the time!

Suddenly aware of Benjy standing there, Paul looked up, his uncombed red hair looking like a stable mop. "What are you doing here?" he demanded.

A crash of thunder kept Benjy from replying. When it was quiet, he said, "I couldn't sleep."

He went in and sat down near Paul.

Paul repeated the question, "What are you doing here?"

Benjy said, "I thought maybe some sweet feed mixed with grain would tempt Cherokee to eat."

Lightning flashed a brilliant white light, and thunder muttered a guttural reply.

"You mean you came out in the middle of a night like this to feed Cherokee?"

"I thought that the extra feeding might help. Then they wouldn't have to ..." His voice trailed off as a howling wind shook the barn.

"He won't eat. Not even carrots."

"You've tried?"

"Again and again. Nobody can help Cherokee now," Paul said sadly.

"I'm sorry."

"Guess you're not such a bad guy after all, superstar."

Benjy jumped up. "Don't call me that!"

"Okay. Okay. Can't you take a joke?"

"Being a jockey means too much to me."

"You really are hung up on the jockey business, aren't you?"

Benjy nodded.

"I think I can help. I know some special things that Danny did to become a jockey. I'll show you."

Before Benjy could reply, thunder boomed overhead like a bass drum. Cherokee raised his head and struggled to his feet. But he was too weak

to stand and he sank into the shavings again.

"This horse means a lot to me," Paul said. His gray eyes brimmed with tears. "Cherokee hates thunder and lightning. That's why I came out to be with him."

This was a side of Paul Benjy had never seen. He

swallowed and said. "He's a good old boy."

"You don't know Cherokee. He's almost blind now, and he can barely stand, but he did a super job for years leading racehorses. He'd go twenty miles at the track each morning. Then he developed bowed tendons in his legs. They almost put him away."

"But Jim saved him?"

Paul nodded. "Dad blistered him by putting a strong liniment on his skin. The heat from the liniment increased circulation to the sore place. After about two years of care, his legs healed."

"Did your mom retrain him?"

"She tried. But he was impossible to control."

Benjy couldn't believe that this gentle old horse had been difficult to retrain as a pleasure horse.

"Dad called the vet. After another physical he found that the bit in his mouth was causing Cherokee terrible pain. Look!" Paul leaned over and held the pony's mouth open.

Part of Cherokee's tongue was missing.

"Someone used a Spanish bit and the wheels tore off half of his tongue," Paul said. "Then any type of bit caused him pain. So Dad used a hackamore—a bridle without a bit. It fit over his nose, and he was beautiful after that."

Again the sound of wind-driven rain hit the wooden roof, and thunder shook the barn. Horses

90

stamped and neighed, some paced the stalls. A horse knocked against a water bucket, and it fell with a great clatter.

Paul said, "As soon as I could sit in a saddle Dad put me up on Cherokee. I loved him right from that moment."

Benjy tried to think of something comforting to say. Cherokee began to tremble. Paul ran into the tack room and returned with a blanket. He gently covered his old horse. But Cherokee shook violently. Paul knelt beside him. Tucking the blanket closer he cried, "Don't die, Cherokee! I don't want you to die!"

Benjy swallowed hard. He wished with all his heart he could do something to help.

Benjy and Paul sat there a long time watching over the old track pony. When the horses quieted in their stalls, Benjy became aware that the storm had moved away. Now the thunder was a distant rumble. Cherokee let out a deep sigh. The trembling stopped, and he settled himself contentedly against Paul. Then he was still.

Paul flung his arms around the horse's neck. His sobs were muffled in Cherokee's mane.

9

You Might Have to Change Your Mind

BENJY FELT a stab in his chest, and his eyes were blurred and watery.

Paul raised his tear-stained face. "He's gone. Cherokee's dead!"

During the next few days things were quiet around the barns. Everyone was sorry for Paul and missed Cherokee. He had been a favorite at Lakeside Farm for many years. Benjy felt a lump in his throat whenever he passed Cherokee's empty stall.

It wasn't until the evening after Cherokee's death that Benjy was able to talk to Jim. Mara was there, too. When Jim heard that Benjy had taught Mara to ride, his eyes filled with anger. Tightening his mouth into a straight line he only said, "Well, what's done is done." And then he walked away.

"I wish Jim had chewed me out," Benjy told

Mara. "He's probably thinking that I'll be going home in a few weeks and he won't have to put up with me anymore."

Mara shook her head glumly.

Although Paul no longer called Benjy superstar, he never again mentioned sharing Danny's jockey secrets. At mealtimes or when they'd meet in the barn, Paul hardly spoke. Benjy wondered if he could have imagined Paul's offer of friendship.

Benjy looked forward to only two things. Jet's cast was coming off on Thursday, and Lori had called a parade planning meeting.

When Benjy arrived at the indoor arena, the other kids were already seated in a circle. Lori said, "When Sara comes, we'll start."

"I'm here," Sara called, coming in behind Benjy. Folding chairs scraped on the floor as everyone made the circle larger to include the newcomers. Benjy noticed that Paul had come and was sitting next to Sherri.

Lori opened the meeting without preliminaries. "We're in big trouble, gang. I heard that the Braeburn Drum and Bugle Corps has a terrific marching group. Their baton twirlers are going to put on an exhibition in front of the judges. They're the state-champion majorettes."

There was a murmur of excited talk. Lori went on, "And the bicycle shop is parading antique bikes, including a high-wheeler with a guy on it doing stunts."

Carmen asked, "Are we still using the circus idea?"

Lori nodded. "But we've got to come up with something smashing to do in front of the judges. We want to win that prize money for equine research. Ideas, anyone?"

When no one offered anything Lori urged, "C'mon, everyone, think! Something different, unique, crazy, whatever!"

The picture of Arcaro sitting on Trouble Seeker's head popped into Benjy's mind. What a sight they would make in the parade!

"I've got it!" he blurted. He described the crow and the horse together. "They'd be spectacular," he concluded.

Carmen agreed, "Neat, real neat."

The praise felt good and Benjy boasted, "Wait until Trouble Seeker trots up to the judges with Arcaro on his head. When my crow says 'Benjy, six o'clock!' and 'It's Mara,' we'll win for sure."

Paul said flatly, "Benjy, nobody here has ever heard Arcaro talk. What makes you think he'll talk now?"

Lori broke in, "And I've been thinking— Trouble Seeker isn't in the parade. We've all been assigned horses."

94

If only he could ride Trouble Seeker in the parade, thought Benjy, but it was impossible. He knew he was lucky that Jim had agreed to let him ride Socks. But he hated to give up his idea and looking at Sherri, he said, "Maybe someone will switch horses and ride Trouble Seeker."

Sherri hesitated. "Trouble is used to crowds because he's been at the track. But I don't want to tackle him. I remember the way he behaved with Mom."

"But he's a different horse now," Benjy said. "He's gentle and obedient, he really is."

"Paul," Sherri asked, "how about you? Want to ride him?"

"Uh-uh, I'm riding Blackjack. Lori and me, we're leading the parade. We have to carry the flags."

Benjy thought of Mara. She'd been making friends with Trouble Seeker, and she was a natural rider. Everyone said so. She could handle Trouble Seeker. And Arcaro would talk in front of Mara. "How about Mara Salamon?" he asked.

"I didn't know she could ride," Lori exclaimed.

"Her mother would absolutely die," Sherri added.

"She's a good rider," Benjy said stubbornly.

"Yes, she is," Sherri agreed.

"Would Jim let her ride Trouble?" Lori asked.

Paul shrugged, and Benjy said, "Let me see what I can do."

Lori nodded. "Well, since we don't have any other ideas, work on it, Benjy. In the meantime, everyone keep thinking. See what you come up with. We'll meet here on our mounts a week from today for parade practice."

The group began to disband. Paul came over to Benjy and said, "Tack up Socks and bring him here. I'll show you how Danny works."

Benjy's heart hammered. He never saddled Socks so quickly. Paul was going to share Danny's secrets with him! When he tripped over a brush he'd dropped on the floor, he told himself to be careful and settle down or he'd lose control of his arms and legs.

Back at the arena after saddling, Paul ordered Benjy to mount.

Did Paul really mean to help?

Paul said, "Do a slow trot, then a fast trot. Put your horse in a right lead."

The directions were given so rapidly that Benjy was flustered.

"Watch your hands!"

Benjy tried again.

"Remember, light hands and a good seat are what you've got to have."

This was old stuff to Benjy. Jim had given him

the same advice long ago. Where were Danny's secrets? Benjy wondered.

"But what about Danny?" he asked Paul.

"Listen. Danny uses Jockey Eddie Arcaro's seat. He read about it in a book." Paul stared at Benjy, tense astride Socks. "But I can see that you aren't ready for Danny's tips. They're too advanced for you."

Benjy's temper flared. He jerked his horse's reins.

"Watch your legs," Paul said evenly. "Quit kicking and calm down, super—I mean, Benjy."

Benjy was too hurt and angry to pay attention to Paul. If Danny's tips came from Eddie Arcaro's book, then Benjy could learn them there by himself. If Danny had other secrets, Paul wasn't going to share them.

Benjy pulled Socks to a sudden stop. He almost slid over the side of the horse. Paul shook his head. "Hey, you trying to buy real estate again? Watch your arms, man."

Benjy dismounted. Paul was backing out on a promise and goading him into a fight. He said angrily, "I've had enough! Leave me alone!"

"Listen," Paul told him. "Want me to give it to you straight? Can you take it?"

Benjy didn't answer. He wasn't interested in anything Paul Spear had to say.

Paul ignored Benjy's silence. "You may be the right size and weight, but you don't have the seat or hands or the feel to be a jockey."

Benjy's throat tightened. He tethered Socks. He wanted to shut the other boy up.

Paul kept talking. "Practice can help. But a jockey needs better than average timing, steady hands, and good reflexes. He's got to work fast under pressure and make correct split-second decisions." Paul paused. "Now take Danny..."

"You take Danny! I've had Danny up to here!" Benjy drew his index finger across his throat.

"Listen, Benjy, I know how much being a jockey means to you. That's why I have to tell you..."

Benjy burst out, "You don't like me! You never liked me. You're still mad because I took Danny's place!"

Paul's eyes met his. "Maybe I was mad at first. Not now. You're okay. That's why I'm telling you like it is. Face it, you're not cut out to be a jockey!"

Paul was saying what Benjy had feared since the first day he'd mounted a horse. He began to shake inside. "I'll be a jockey, or else!" he shouted.

"Man, are you a blockhead! You might just have to change your blockhead mind."

Benjy's hands clenched into fists. Without another word he swung hard at Paul's nose.

Paul ducked, grabbed Benjy's arms, and held him. "I didn't come to fight. You're going to listen whether you want to or not."

Benjy was breathing hard. He wanted to throw another punch, but he couldn't break out of Paul's grasp.

Paul said, "You saw how a jockey works at the track. Jockeys must have good muscle control. Your arms and legs are all over the place."

Benjy pictured Danny riding in the fifth race at Arlington. He and Calico Kate were in perfect rhythm racing down the backstretch for the finish wire. He remembered the doubts he'd had about becoming a jockey that day.

Suddenly Benjy stopped struggling against Paul. The older boy relaxed his grip and stepped back cautiously, watching.

Benjy's face was flushed. He kicked at the straw under his feet. It was not easy to admit that what Paul had said made sense. He'd suspected it himself during the first days on the farm. Jockey or else? This was the end of his dreams.

"Paul! Benjy!" It was Sherri's voice, and they knew something was wrong.

"Come quick! Trouble Seeker fell into a ditch in front of Mara's house, and he can't get out!"

10
Benjy to the Rescue

PAUL RAN OUT with Sherri. Benjy locked Socks in his stall and raced to Mara's.

Mara, Paul, Sherri, and several of the Lakeside kids were gathered around the freshly dug ditch where the house sewer was being repaired. The ditch ran from the Salamon house to the street.

Trouble Seeker lay in the narrow excavation, up to his belly in mud. He thrashed frantically, trying to get to his feet, and nickered in shrill tones when he failed.

Mara said, "Poor Trouble Seeker. It's a good thing that Mom isn't home yet."

"What happened?" Benjy asked.

"Trouble was grazing near the lake with the other horses," Lori said. "Someone left the gate open, and he walked out."

Sherri added, "And before he was missed, he'd

eaten his way to the Salamon house and fallen into the ditch.''

Benjy saw hoofprints marking Trouble Seeker's patch across the beautifully kept lawn.

"Maybe we can lift him out by his halter," suggested Mara.

"No way," said Paul. "That mud is like quicksand. He's sinking every minute. Sherri, did you call Dad?"

"He's coming."

Arcaro flew by and hovered around Trouble Seeker, cawing and scolding. He perched on a tree branch to watch over his friend.

The blue pickup arrived, and Trouble Seeker whinnied furiously when he saw Jim and Linda.

Paul asked, "Can we buckle a rope to his halter and pull him out?"

Jim shook his head. "The halter would probably break." He turned to Sherri. "Go into Mara's and call Dr. Egel. Tell him to get over here—quick!"

Trouble Seeker moved his head from side to side. He struggled to stand, but he couldn't. Finally exhausted, he lay quiet, his eyes filled with fright.

Jim said, "I've got an idea. Paul, bring me the gunnysacks from the truck and the ropes. Benjy, go to the barn and get two girths."

When Benjy returned, Jim put the girths

together. He smoothed the gunnysacks in place under Trouble's forelegs and tied the girths around them. Then he hooked on a strong rope.

"Okay, kids, we're going to lift Trouble. Linda, Paul, Sherri—line up behind me. Benjy, Mara, Lori, next. Then Carmen, Sara, and Anne."

Two boys who had been watching asked if they could help.

"We need everyone we can get," Jim said. "Okay, hold the rope. Ready? Pull!"

It was the hardest tug-of-war Benjy had ever taken part in—Lakeside Farm against the muddy ditch. But as hard as Jim, Linda, and the kids pulled, they couldn't lift the Thoroughbred.

Trouble Seeker's nickers turned to groans. His eyes looked frantic.

Jim said, "Everyone in place. We'll try again."

Once more they pulled together.

"Again!" commanded Jim. "Once again." Benjy's hands were raw from the rope. Sweat was streaming down Jim's face. "We're not even budging him."

Linda took out a handkerchief and wiped her neck. The kids flopped on the ground, breathing heavily.

Arcaro, extremely agitated, flew down flapping his wings and cawing loudly as he circled his friend in the ditch.

102

The noise and excitement had attracted a crowd of neighbors. "The poor horse is sinking!" one woman said.

"They'll never get him out!" added a man.

Dr. Egel drove up in his mobile veterinarian unit. "I got your call on my car phone, Jim. Luckily I was nearby at Arlington Park. Where is he?"

Jim pointed to Trouble Seeker in the ditch.

Dr. Egel whistled.

Jim told him how they'd tried to lift Trouble Seeker. The doctor paced the ditch, looking thoughtful. "I don't know how we can pull that horse out." He glanced at the Thoroughbred. "But I do know that he can't last there much longer."

The crowd whispered in hushed tones, sensing how serious the situation was. A man said, "Maybe they'll have to shoot him."

Shivers shook Benjy. They couldn't shoot Trouble Seeker! He was a young, healthy horse, and some day Benjy was going to ride him. Trouble had to be saved!

Suddenly Benjy recalled a car back home that had fallen into a ditch where the gas company had been working.

"Jim!" Benjy blurted, "I saw a tow truck with a winch pull a car out of a ditch. And a car is heavier than a horse."

Jim and Dr. Egel exchanged looks. The vet said, "It's worth a try."

Linda spoke urgently. "The Braeburn Standard Station is only a mile away. They have a tow truck."

"I'll look up the number." Mara ran toward her house.

Sherri called, "Tell them it's an emergency."

When Mara returned she said, "They'll be right over."

It was a long fifteen minutes. Dr. Egel gave Trouble Seeker a shot to quiet him, and the Thoroughbred's eyes took on a glassy look.

"I hope he hasn't broken a leg," said Dr. Egel.

A chugging sound announced the tow truck's arrival, and everyone tensed. Arcaro flew to his treetop. A bearded young man in khaki jumped out.

"Hurry," Jim said. "We don't know how much longer this horse can last."

The young man surveyed the situation.

"Can you pull him out?" Jim asked.

"We'll try. Secure the ropes around the horse. I'll back up the truck as close to the ditch as possible."

Jim checked the gunnysacks, cinches, and ropes, making sure they were in place.

The man pulled a cable from the truck, and

handed the cable to Jim. "Hold it tight until the winch takes over." Then he went back to the truck and started the winch.

Benjy's heart pounded in his throat as the winch began to turn. Dr. Egel watched Trouble Seeker carefully as the wire uncoiled. Slowly, very slowly, Trouble was moving. Benjy was relieved to see the horse's legs come up out of the ditch.

Jim said, "Keep going."

Inches at a time, the horse was raised from the ditch. The winch creaked under its heavy burden, and Benjy's heart plummeted to his boots. Would the winch hold? There was just a little more to go. Creak! Creak!

The winch held.

"He's out!" Benjy shouted.

The crowd cheered. Trouble Seeker lay on the ground, looking dazed, his entire body, including his white star, covered with mud. He looked more like a black than a chestnut horse. Arcaro flew down and circled his friend. Then he retreated to the top branch of the tree.

"Mara, do you have a garden hose?" Jim asked.

Jim hosed Trouble Seeker while he lay on the ground. The cold water revived him. His coat glistened wet and reddish again. He stood up on shaky feet and shook off the water, showering everyone. The crowd laughed and moved back.

"That's right. Give him room," ordered Dr. Egel. He examined Trouble Seeker's legs. "He's in good shape."

The driver said, "I've seen a horse tow a truck, but this is the first time my truck towed a horse!" He grinned and drove off.

Benjy hugged Trouble Seeker. The horse rubbed against him, spotting his T-shirt and nosing his cap off. Benjy smiled and picked up his cap. Then he hooked a lead rope to Trouble's halter.

"See you all tomorrow morning around eight," said the veterinarian. "We'll take off Jet's cast."

"Thanks for coming," Jim said.

"Don't thank me. The winch probably saved your horse's life."

Benjy was happy. At last he'd done something right. But his happiness faded, and his heart hammered in his chest when he saw Mrs. Salamon's car approaching. What would she do when she saw her lawn?

"Darn Mara's mother!" Paul said at breakfast the next morning.

Sherri served a pile of French toast. "Mara cried all night," she put in. "But she couldn't talk her mother out of it. Their attorney is preparing the petition to prohibit horses in Braeburn."

Jim said dejectedly, "Mrs. Salamon warned us that if one of our horses ever again damaged her property she'd take legal means to get us to move."

Linda sighed. "We really can't blame her after what happened to her garden. And now her lawn is ruined."

"But the kids offered to repair the lawn," Benjy protested.

Paul asked, "What'll happen if they get the required number of signatures on the petition?"

"They'll bring the matter before the city council," said Linda.

"And there are plenty of anti-horse people there," Jim said.

"Oh, Daddy, what'll we do?" Sherri cried.

Before Jim could reply, Dr. Egel opened the door and put his head in. "Morning, folks. Has anyone fallen in a ditch today?"

"Hi, doc, want a cup of coffee?" Linda asked.

"No, thanks. I've had breakfast. I'm going to take off Jet's cast now."

Everyone jumped up but Sherri, who was on kitchen duty. As they walked to the barn, Dr. Egel said to Jim, "I examined Trouble Seeker earlier. His little escapade didn't hurt him one bit."

"Well, it hurt us," Jim said. He told the veterinarian about Mrs. Salamon's petition.

Dr. Egel said, "I can understand how Mrs. Salamon feels, but Lakeside Farm was here before she was. And look at all the happy kids around here. Are the neighbors on her side?"

Jim shrugged. "Not the parents of our riders, but plenty of others. It might mean a drastic change in our lives."

"I'm sorry, Jim."

"We'll wait and see," Jim said. "Now I'm interested in Jet. Benjy, bring the mare into the aisle, please."

Dr. Egel gave her a shot to keep her quiet. Then he said, "Benjy, take the lead chain and hold Jet's head. Talk to her. She trusts you."

The cast cutter vibrated up and down. Dr. Egel

worked quickly and expertly making a groove in the cast. He was careful not to cut the horse's skin.

When the groove was cut, the veterinarian put down the saw and took out the cast spreader.

Jet nickered and moved her head. "Keep cool, Jet," Benjy said, stroking her neck. "It's almost over."

The cast spreader was like a pliers, but it worked in reverse. The doctor put the spreader in the groove he'd made with the cutter and spread the cast.

"Just a few more minutes," Benjy said soothingly.

The cast spread very little at first. Then the doctor stuck his fingers in, making the groove wider and wider. Finally Jet's leg was free.

The leg was enlarged, but not puffy. "It looks good," said Dr. Egel. "We'll keep a bandage on it for five days. A fresh one each day. Okay, Benjy?"

Benjy nodded.

Dr. Egel explained, "It'll give her extra support. But after three days, just put the bandage on at night. I don't want her to be dependent on it."

Jim asked, "What about massage?"

"Massage the leg an hour a day with mild liniment."

Paul asked, "Can we walk her in the paddock or take her to the lake?"

"Walking is good for her. Water is helpful, too, for loosening her muscles."

"When can I start retraining her?" Linda asked.

"In about six months. She'll probably swing that leg when she runs because her ankle won't flex. But she's sound. Your mare's had excellent care, Jim."

Everyone looked at Benjy. It felt good to get a compliment from Dr. Egel. But Benjy wished the praise had been given for his riding, instead.

When Jet had been squared away, Benjy saddled Socks and went into the back arena. He didn't expect Mara to show up today, but when he arrived she was waiting.

Tears filled her eyes. "Oh, Benjy. I thought you weren't coming. I didn't know if you'd ever let me ride again."

"Nobody here blames you for what happened, Mara. You've got to keep riding."

When Benjy saw Mara in the saddle, he once again wished that he could ride as well as she. After the practice session, Mara dismounted and said, "When you become a famous jockey, I'll tell everyone that you were my teacher."

Mara's words jolted him. He'd never be a jockey, he realized that, but he didn't tell Mara. He had something else on his mind. "Mara, I want to ask you a favor. It's very important."

110

"I owe you plenty. What is it?"

"Will you ride Trouble Seeker in the Labor Day Parade?"

Mara grimaced.

"I know you can handle him."

"I'm not afraid of Trouble Seeker. But my mother never misses a parade. She sits in the grandstand with the judges. My dad is on the city council."

Benjy's hopes were now a heap of rubbish.

"Ask me something else. Anything!"

Benjy thought, what more could Mara's mother do to Jim and Linda than she'd already done? "Mara, the petition against horses is going to be circulated, so what harm would it do if you rode in the parade? At least the kids will have a chance to win the money for equine research."

Mara considered the idea. "Did Jim or Linda say I could ride Trouble Seeker?'

"Not yet. But I'm sure they'll give you permission after they see you ride."

She hesitated, and Benjy held his breath.

"Okay," Mara said slowly, "I'll do it for the kids."

"Yippee!" Benjy yelled so loud that Socks turned his head at the hitching post. "Here's our plan." Benjy told Mara about the circus theme and about his idea to have Arcaro perch on Trouble

Seeker's head. "When Arcaro says 'Ben-nn-njy! It's six o'clock!' in front of the judges, we'll win!"

"Whoa!" Mara raised her ·hand. "Back up, Benjy. Arcaro hates strangers and crowds."

Mara was right. Benjy remembered that when Trouble Seeker was in the ditch, the noise of the spectators had sent Arcaro hiding in a tree. "I'll think of something. I've got almost three weeks."

How could he get Arcaro to talk in front of a crowd? Benjy thought about it for days. One evening, just two weeks before parade time, the solution came to him. He was watching a baseball game on TV when he remembered what Jim had told him about how trainers accustomed race-horses to noise. That was it! He'd put Arcaro in a room with the TV blasting every day during the ball game. Then the crow would get used to the sound of a loudspeaker and crowds yelling. That was the way they taught young racehorses in the shed row at Arlington.

The next day, Benjy put Arcaro in his carrier and placed him on a table directly in front of the TV. Arcaro didn't like being cooped up. He scolded and cawed raucously. And when Benjy turned on the TV, Arcaro cowered in the corner, hiding his head.

"You'll get used to it," Benjy told his pet.

11
Arcaro Stops the Show

AFTER A WEEK in front of the TV, Arcaro seemed accustomed to the noisy ball games. Benjy hoped that now his crow would talk before a crowd. At rehearsals, although Arcaro rode happily on Trouble Seeker's head, Benjy still couldn't persuade the crow to speak. He worked patiently with Arcaro until the day of the parade and hoped for the best.

On Labor Day there was a gay circus atmosphere in the yard. Costumed performers moved about in a confusion of color, noise, and glitter dust. Beribboned horses with gold and silver hooves pawed the ground. The horses' nickers added to the commotion. The odors of glue, hair spray, and saddle soap hung on the humid late summer air.

Linda came out. "Benjy, hurry into your clown costume and report to the back arena for makeup."

In his room, Benjy put on the top of his costume—Paul's large white sweat shirt. Benjy had sewn red yarn tassels down the front. Arcaro, in his carrier, pecked at the mesh screen and cawed furiously. His large eyes beseeched Benjy to let him out.

"Later, Arcaro," Benjy said. He put on the red crepe-paper collar. Then he slipped on his white jeans and tucked the pant legs into white socks.

Benjy reached for the white cotton stocking hat, pulled it over his hair, and topped the hat with his faded red jockey cap. He pinned on a button that said, "Give to Equine Research." White cotton gloves completed his costume. Benjy looked into the mirror and smiled. "Hi, clown."

Arcaro squawked, "Ben-nn-njy! Ben-nn-njy!"

"Save that for later, Arcaro."

When Benjy entered the arena, a voice called, "Over here for clown alley, Benjy." The voice was Sherri's but it came from a baggy-pants clown with a red rubber-ball nose.

Benjy grinned. "You look neat, Sherri."

"Thanks," Sherri said. Then she worked on Benjy's face with clown white, eyebrow pencil and lipstick. She finished with a big red smear of a mouth, stretching from ear to ear.

In the yard, Lori blew a whistle which hung around her neck. "Ten minutes!"

Everyone started moving faster. They put last minute touches on their costumes and bridled their horses. Benjy wondered where Mara was. He had a sudden fear that she wouldn't show up. He sighed with relief when she came into the yard, leading Trouble Seeker.

Mara wore a spangled shirt with a bright sash, but her face was hidden under a large floppy hat. It wouldn't be easy for her mother to recognize her.

"That's a neat clown outfit, Benjy," Mara said.

Benjy was pleased that Mara liked his costume. "You don't look so bad yourself," he replied.

"Will you hold Socks, please, Mara? I'll get Arcaro."

When Benjy returned Mara said, "I'm scared."

"About riding Trouble Seeker?"

"No. I can handle him."

"Then what?"

"About my mother. And I'm wondering if Arcaro will talk after all."

Benjy said, "I sure hope he will." He opened the carrier and placed Arcaro on Trouble Seeker's head. The Thoroughbred cocked his head as if to welcome his friend.

"Listen, Arcaro," Benjy said. "We're pinning all our hopes on you."

The crow fluttered his wings and hopped up and down.

Mara asked, "Do you think he'll talk?"

"He's got to," Benjy replied. "He's just got to."

Paul came out, wearing a fluffy white moustache, a goatee, and glittering cowboy clothes. Waving a crop, he shouted, "Move 'em out!" He was the circus clown captain.

Lori wore a long blue cape and looked like a princess. Jon and David Kirsch were dressed as Chinese jugglers, and Steve Gutterman, the animal trainer, carried a stuffed tiger. Carmen was an acrobat in red tights, and Sara wore a beautiful pink ballet costume.

Trouble Seeker lowered his head and bucked. Benjy, riding behind, hoped that Mara wouldn't lose control. She spoke to Trouble soothingly, and the Thoroughbred stayed in his place.

As they rode toward the street, Benjy thought about Mara's mother. When she saw Mara riding Trouble Seeker what would she say? What might she do? Benjy was the one who had talked Mara into riding the racehorse in the parade. Maybe he shouldn't have done it.

And what if Arcaro wouldn't talk after all?

Lakeside Farm lined up behind the bicycle shop float. They fell into step to the tune of "Anchors Aweigh" blasted by the Braeburn Drum and Bugle Corps.

A crowd stood on the sidewalk, three-deep. It

116

seemed to Benjy that every resident of Braeburn was at the parade.

The horses stepped sprightly to the music. Benjy bounced up and down in the saddle. Even Socks, the old track pony, was hard to hold down. The parade wound through the business district, past the library, and into the heart of town. Loud cries of "Here come the clowns!" rang out. Wherever they marched, spectators waved and applauded. Parents held their children up to see Benjy or to shake hands.

Once Arcaro flew off into a tree and Benjy panicked. But he soon came back to his perch between Trouble Seeker's ears.

The parade turned toward the city hall and the grandstand. It was jammed with council members and judges. Benjy spied Linda and Jim sitting in the exhibitors' area.

Lori called a halt while the majorettes ahead of Lakeside performed. The baton twirlers were champs and they showed it. Would Lakeside's presentation equal theirs? Benjy felt sweat on his chest and under his arms. The clown costume was making him very warm.

Lori blew the whistle. It was Lakeside's turn in front of the grandstand. Paul cried, "Welcome to the greatest show on earth!" Benjy's belly knotted.

The crowd watched attentively as the Chinese

117

jugglers on horseback whirled hoops on their arms. Then Carmen, riding bareback, jumped off and on her horse again, amid loud applause.

Now it was Mara's turn. She stopped Trouble Seeker in front of the grandstand. Benjy, the whiteface clown, pretended to fall off his horse. Sherri, the baggy-pants clown, jumped off to save him. Benjy handed her Socks's reins. Her baggy pants began to slip. Then her nose lit up, and everyone laughed and clapped.

Arcaro cawed excitedly and jumped up and down.

Someone yelled, "Look at that crow on the horse's head!"

Every eye in the grandstand was on Arcaro.

Benjy said loudly, "Here's Arcaro, the talking crow!"

Mara whispered, "That's my mom in the pink slack suit. She hasn't seen me yet. Oh, please make Arcaro talk."

Benjy's legs began to shake. After all his promises to the kids, Arcaro just had to talk! He lunged for the crow, and fell over his own feet. He was too embarrassed to look toward the grandstand when he got up. To make matters worse, Trouble Seeker nudged off his cap.

In the middle of the act!

But everyone was clapping and laughing. They

118

thought it was part of the show. A voice yelled, "Did you see that horse push off the clown's cap?"

Benjy reached for his cap, but he wasn't quick enough. Arcaro swooped down on it, picked it up in his beak and flew into the reviewing stand. He perched on the table near the microphone with the cap held out as if asking for money. People nearby read the button, "Give to Equine Research," and put money in. Even the announcer dug into his pockets for coins. He was laughing too hard to speak.

Arcaro, enjoying the attention, looked around as if to say, "I'm the greatest!"

Suddenly a woman in the grandstand rose and screamed, "It's Mara!" It was Mrs. Salamon.

Arcaro dropped the cap on the table and his scratchy voice came over the loudspeaker amplified a thousand times. "It's Mara! It's Mara!"

"That crow talks, too!" cried the announcer.

The crowd went wild, including the kids from Lakeside Farm. Even Mara's mother broke into laughter—she couldn't help it.

"Good going, Arcaro," Benjy heard Jim say.

But there was no stopping Arcaro now. He cawed into the loudspeaker, "Ben-nn-njy! Ben-nn-njy! Six o'clock!"

"Time!" gasped the announcer.

Benjy ran up, emptied the money into his pocket, and put on his jockey cap. Arcaro hopped on his shoulder.

"You were super," Benjy declared.

Amidst applause, Benjy mounted Socks, and Lakeside Farm marched off to wait for the announcement of the winner.

When all the floats and marchers had passéd the grandstand, the crowd was hushed and expectant. Benjy could barely breathe. But whether they'd won or not, Arcaro had done a fine job.

The loudspeaker crackled, and the announcer said, "Ladies and gentlemen, this has been one of the best parades in Braeburn's history. All of the floats and marchers are to be congratulated. But the judges have decided that there is one entry that deserves the $100 prize. That's Lakeside Farm and their favorite charity, the Association for Equine Research."

There was a roar of approval. Paul yelled to Benjy, "You did it!" Everyone applauded and cheered as Lori rode up and accepted the money for equine research.

Benjy felt like turning a clown cartwheel right in the street. And he almost did. But he froze in the saddle when he saw Mrs. Salamon pushing through the crowd toward them. She called, "Mara, I want to talk to you!"

12
Goodbye to Lakeside

BENJY WANTED to protect Mara from her mother's anger, but he felt helpless. Why couldn't Mrs. Salamon accept the fact that Mara loved riding?

"Mother!" Mara exclaimed and dismounted, handing the reins to Benjy. She straightened her shoulders and faced her mother. "I've been riding all summer," she said. "I love horses! I've got to ride!"

"She's a natural!" Benjy said.

Lori agreed. "She's great!"

Mrs. Salamon stared at Mara and her friends. Then she caught her breath and reached out toward Mara. "I didn't know!" she said. "I didn't know until today how much riding means to you. I—I'm proud of you, I guess." And there stood Mara and her mother hugging each other. It was

hard to tell whether they were laughing or crying.

Benjy felt a wave of homesickness. He wished his parents had been in the grandstand, cheering for him. But now Mara was pulling Benjy over to meet her mother. Mrs. Salamon said, "When I saw Mara riding that beautiful Thoroughbred I realized what a fine rider she is. I loved horses once, too, but I had a bad experience. I didn't want Mara to be hurt that way. Now I see how wrong that was. I should have given her a chance to ride."

Then Mara said, "The Lakeside Farm people are good neighbors after all, aren't they, Mom? Nobody will make them move, will they?"

Mrs. Salamon said, "We'll forget about the petition. I'll call my lawyer first thing in the morning."

"Oh, Mom, you're the greatest!" Mara hugged her mother again.

Now Mara mounted Trouble Seeker and waving to her mother, she and Benjy clopped down the street. They couldn't wait to tell Jim and Linda the good news.

The next afternoon before dinner, Benjy was in his room packing. It didn't take long to stuff his shirts, jeans, and other things into his duffel bag. He put in his scrapbook and Eddie Arcaro's book, *I Ride To Win!* That book still meant a lot to him.

Where was everybody? It was very quiet. Since

he'd be catching the bus for Chicago at five o'clock in the morning, Benjy decided to say goodbye to the horses now. In the yard, he whistled for Arcaro. The crow flew out and perched on his shoulder.

"Well, Arcaro," he said, "we're going home."

"You bet!" squawked the crow.

Benjy went into the small blue barn first and said goodbye to Julep, Magic, and the privately owned horses. He gave them each a carrot. Then he walked quickly to the large barn. His boot heels clicked on the wooden planking as he went from one stall to the next on Sherri's side of the barn, saying his farewells and giving carrots. The horses nickered their thanks.

Now it was time for the left side of the barn, his side. There was a hard knot in Benjy's throat. "Bye Socks," Benjy said. The horse whinnied when he heard his voice. "I owe you a lot. You taught me to ride." He stroked the little palomino's neck. "You are the most patient horse I know."

He moved on. "Take care, Jet. Your leg is getting better every day. You'll soon be good as new." The mare stuck her head out and nuzzled Benjy's shoulder. She'd learned to trust him.

There was a sharp pain when Benjy reached Cherokee's empty stall. He thought about the game little track pony with half a tongue. "I won't forget you, Cherokee," he said softly.

He came to Trouble Seeker last. The horse shoved his nose toward Benjy. Arcaro cawed loudly and perched between his friend's ears. Trouble whinnied as if he were laughing.

Benjy ran his hand across the horse's velvet-soft nostrils and thought about how Trouble Seeker had been rescued from the ditch. He'd probably never see the handsome chestnut with the white star again.

The thought made his eyes fill with tears. He slid open the stall door and cried, "Trouble Seeker!" Then he wrapped his arms around the horse's neck and sobbed like a little kid.

After a while, Benjy closed the stall door, ran down to the lake, and stretched out on the grass. Arms under his head, he stared dry eyed at the sky.

What was the matter with him? He loved his home in the city, and he was looking forward to seeing his parents and friends. But he loved Lakeside Farm, too. Now that he was leaving, he was aware of every nicker and neigh from the barns, the sweet smell of the grass in the pasture, the warmth of the horses' bodies. He'd come here in June with high hopes. Jockey, or else! Well, he'd found out that he wasn't meant to be a jockey.

Benjy thought about the talk he'd had with Jim last night. He'd told Jim how disappointed he was that he'd never be a jockey like Danny. Jim had replied, "Well, Danny is Danny. And he's a darn good jockey. But Benjy, you're on your way to being a fine horseman. You've done a great job with Jet. And you're a good teacher, too. Look at how well Mara performed on Trouble Seeker." Jim smiled. "And what a way you have with animals and birds!"

Then Jim had put his hand on Benjy's shoulder and said, "Linda and I think you've grown a lot this summer. In fact, you've grown in more ways than one. Step on that scale, right now, sir."

Benjy had jumped on the scale. "I've gained five pounds!"

Jim laughed. "Stand against the wall. You've also grown two inches! Now I have to look up to you!"

Benjy grinned.

"You'd better think about being a veterinarian or a teacher. There are lots of horse jobs for tall guys."

The dinner gong broke into Benjy's thoughts. How long had he been lying there? He jumped up and whistled for Arcaro. The crow flew out of the barn and perched on Benjy's shoulder. "Let's go," said Benjy, giving Arcaro a pat.

They headed toward the house. As Benjy opened the kitchen door a burst of voices yelled, "Surprise!"

Benjy's heart pounded. A party for him! No wonder there had been nobody around this afternoon. The kitchen was decorated with colored streamers and a huge sign said "We'll miss you, Benjy."

Linda was at the stove, wearing a blue-checked apron over her jeans. Jim, Paul, Sherri, and Mara smiled as Lori and the other kids came up and clapped him on the back.

Seated at the dinner table with all his friends, Benjy felt special. When they'd eaten dessert, Jim rose and said, "I hate speeches, but because it's Benjy's last night, I'm going to make one."

"Hear! Hear!" everyone shouted.

"First, I want to report that Mrs. Salamon has withdrawn her petition against horses, and Lakeside Farm hopes to be in business for a long time."

Loud cheers filled the kitchen.

"Second, we've contributed the sum of $108.26 to the Association for Equine Research. You all know who solicited the $8.26."

The kids pounded the table and yelled, "Yea, Arcaro!"

Arcaro flapped his wings, circled the kitchen ceiling, and zoomed down on Benjy's shoulder.

Jim held up his hand. "Last but not least, for Linda, Paul, Sherri, and me, we want to tell Benjy how much we've enjoyed having him as part of our family." Jim turned to Benjy, "And you and Arcaro are invited back to Lakeside Farm next summer."

Benjy's face hurt from grinning. He'd never heard so much clapping, whistling, and stomping. Then Paul shouted, "Speech! Speech!"

Benjy stood up and everyone grew quiet. He swallowed hard and said, "I've made some great friends this summer, both two-footed and four-footed." He looked around the table at the smiling faces. "Last June I wanted to be a jockey more than anything in the world." He turned toward Paul. "I know now that there are many things that I can do with horses. You all made me see that. So I'll be back next summer to find out what's best for me."

Arcaro hopped up and down on Benjy's shoulder and thrust out his neck. "You bet! You bet!" he squawked.